PRESENT WOMAN
NARKIS ALON

PRESENT WOMAN

Our pleasure, Our power

NARKIS ALON

PRESENT WOMAN
NARKIS ALON

Copyright © 2023 by Narkis Alon
All rights reserved

All rights reserved. No part of this book may be reproduced, scanned or distributed in any printed or electronic form without permission. Please do not participate in or encourage piracy of copyrighted materials in violation of the author's rights. Purchase only authorized editions.

All names used in the text are pseudonyms and situations changed in order to protect true identities.

Originally translated by:
Leanna Raday

Edited by:
Dalia Rosenfeld

Cover illustration by:
Hulya Ozdemir

Cover design by:
Oksana Kravtsova

DEDICATION

This book is dedicated to all the people who made it possible.

To Alon, my love, who helped me get to know myself as a sexual entity and, by so doing, made me Lavie and Agam's mother, and who has agreed to expose himself in these pages with the hope that our story might help others.

To my mother, who taught me everything I know about femininity. To my father, who taught me excellence and the joy of creation.

To my sisters, who taught me feminine solidarity, and to my partners in Double-You, who have practiced this work with me for many years.

To all the other people who agreed to participate in this project, even under aliases. I trust that your generosity and courage will benefit the readers of this book and their loved ones.

And of course – thank you! All of you who have decided to read this book.

There are three ways to experience this book:
You can simply read it.
You can read it while writing your own personal story in the notebook available in the QR code below.
You can share your story with others.

Scan the QR code for a detailed explanation.

www.narkisalon.com/booklet-en

May it be a fruitful journey that connects you to your body.

CONTENTS

CHAPTER 0
Context / Short biography 9

CHAPTER 1
So This Is What an Orgasm Is All About! 21

CHAPTER 2
Opening Gates 43

CHAPTER 3
Why Are You Closing Up? 63

CHAPTER 4
I Also Wanted to Open Up Like a Flower 81

CHAPTER 5
Teach Me How to Be a Strong Woman 111

CHAPTER 6
Encountering the Beast 139

CHAPTER 7
Present Women 171

CHAPTER 8
Man and Woman 191

APPENDIX. SPACES TO VISIT AFTER READING 207

THANKS & RECOMMENDATIONS 211

CHAPTER 0
CONTEXT / SHORT BIO

I'M FIVE, surrounded by the comforts of a loving family, but during the day my parents are at work and my older sisters busy playing with their friends. Home alone, I play with my imaginary ones and we embark on journeys that transform the rooms of our apartment into a wonderful new world. A special character accompanies me throughout: an all-powerful woman, a kind-hearted version of Ursula from *The Little Mermaid*, who generously introduces me to her friends before our adventures begin. Every now and then my sister Nilli stops what she's doing and says to me: "Stop talking to yourself already!"

At night I dream intense dreams. I am floating in space, standing in the middle of the ocean, meeting people who are no longer alive. In kindergarten, I share my stories with whoever is willing to listen. To the circle of girls around me I tell of my adventures in the Land of the Barbies.

One day I promise Yael that I'll take her there. Her father brings her over and I take them on a walk. When we reach the steep path to the park I explain that the cloud stairs that lead to the Land of the Barbies descend from the patch of sky above.

"And where are they now?" Yael's father asks me.

"I don't know," I reply.

He turns to his daughter and says, "Yael, it's just like I told you — there is no such thing. It's all in her imagination." Yael bursts into tears and stops talking to me. The next day at kindergarten everyone calls me a liar.

I'M THIRTEEN. I meet Ohad, who goes to a different school, and we become a couple. He smokes cigarettes and listens to grownup music. He has a low voice, as if he's already a man. From the shaggy rug in his room, he plays a song for me: "Quit smoking already, quit smoking already." We laugh, he takes my hand and invites me to follow him. We lie down next to each other on his bed. He touches me. I lie on top of him and he starts moving from side to side, rubbing against me.

"What are you doing?" I ask.

"Dry sex," he replies.

Through our clothes, his genitals meet mine. Does this feel good? I ask myself. Not really. Should I move? Stay put? My body is frozen, my brain racing every which way. Ohad breathes heavily, then turns his head to one side and eases me off him. We're both lying on our backs. He turns his head toward me and gives me a half-smile.

I'M FIFTEEN. I've got an eating disorder and spend most of my time thinking about boys and what they think about me.

I'm part of a group of high school girls who are considered the "hot" girls of Tel Aviv. This is expressed by spending our evenings with seniors. Each of us is sexually involved with one of them, if not more.

I hope Yarden notices me. A year ago he was my troop leader.

I spend all of summer camp trying to get his attention. He's indifferent to me, which makes me fall even harder for him. On the last night, he asks if I want to sleep with him in his hammock. I'm so excited. We hold hands as we swing back and forth.

We close our eyes, as if trying to sleep, and then his hand starts gliding across my body. As things get more intense, I do what I do best in situations like these — freeze. He feels me up for a while, then moves down my stomach until he reaches my genitals. He touches me over my underpants. It's neither pleasant nor unpleasant, mainly embarrassing. Before I can decide what to do, he gently takes my hand and puts it on his penis. This is my first encounter with male genitals. I stroke his penis as he tries to guide me. My hand moves at his instruction. At one point I realize that he's stopped moving. I open my eyes and see that he's fallen asleep. My heart is pounding. I have achieved my goal. I think I'm in a relationship with Yarden. The next day he even hugs me in public, and I feel like a princess.

After camp is over, we talk once in a while. He doesn't express any feelings for me. He occasionally sends messages, inviting me over. One day I discover that he's also in a relationship with another girl in our gang. They both deny it.

Ever since I was a little girl I've been able to tell my mom anything. Hearing one story about Yarden is enough for her to say: "He sounds like a boy with issues. Stay away from men with issues — they'll ruin your life."

I'M SIXTEEN. I get excellent grades on my finals. I'm also more involved in the scouts, becoming the instructor for a deaf autistic child and leading large-scale volunteer projects. During the summer vacation before my junior year I start working at a bar called The Red Bar. It's a dimly-lit place on an alley off Nahalat Binyamin, a pedestrian street packed with people. Those lucky enough to arrive early sit at tables laden with beer and edamame or fries. Balancing drinks, I make my way through the multitude. I smile at some, hi-five or hug others, experiencing a sense of belonging with this Tel Aviv group of regulars.

When it gets late, only the really wasted customers stick around. Sometimes, one of them throws up and I go run for a rag. The other waitresses call me "Narki" (a play on words combining Narkis and "*Ki*," the word for vomit in Hebrew). And the men—eternal bachelors in their forties who call this place home—hang on until 4 A.M.. While we wipe down the tables and chairs before closing, they sit by the bar and hit on us relentlessly; it comes with the job.

One evening, a poet named Jacob hands me a napkin with a poem he has written for me. He kisses me. He stinks but I kiss him back, because no one has ever written me a poem before.

I'm seventeen, I go to an event at the home of one of my youth group friends.

I'm in high spirits, wearing a blue dress with green polka dots. I sit down at the table next to my friend. I don't know most of the people there; one of the guys keeps telling stupid jokes, and there's something about his style that I like. I'm the only one who laughs, and loudly. He tells my friend that he's in love with me and asks for my number. A few weeks later we're a couple.

It's the first time a man has professed his love to me and given me the attention associated with the title "girlfriend." He's also the first man I sleep with. It hurts and I don't enjoy it, but I keep quiet. When he asks if everything is OK, I smile and pretend it is. We're together for almost two years. We're good friends, but at one point I start avoiding any sexual encounters with him. He stops trying, the relationship dies and we break up.

I'M 21 and out of the army after serving in an intelligence unit. Making good money in business development for a startup, I wear my mother's clothes to meetings so that the clients don't ask how old I am.

When my bosses are pleased I'm happy. When they're disappointed, I'm sad. Most of the time they're pleased, because I bring good leads, but sometimes they silence me at meetings with cynical or demeaning remarks. I have to bite my lip to stop myself from crying.

I have a boyfriend, Lior. He is the first man I confide in: I don't enjoy sex. He cares about me and wants to help. He takes on our intimate relations as his pet project. He tells me how much he loves to fall asleep after sex with his penis still inside—"it's so natural." When he says this, he smiles in a way that implies that it'll happen to us too, he'll bring me there. He goes very slowly, maintaining eye contact and making sure that everything is OK, but it still hurts. Lior tries so hard to make it work that I don't want to let him down. I hang in there until he comes, and then politely try to get him out of me. He says "a little longer," "try to let go," and hugs me with a warmth and sweetness that paralyze me. Sometimes he stays inside me for more than an hour afterwards, which only makes me even more frozen. At one point he realizes that I'm still not enjoying myself and feels uncomfortable continuing to have sex with me. We break up after a year, in a friendly way. I always break up in a friendly way.

I'M 22. I decide to go on a long post-army trip abroad. I tell my boss I'll be back in two months and he promises to keep my job.

I go backpacking in Central America, travelling between guesthouses. Until then, I have only had sex with two men who were my boyfriends at the time. I've never had a one-night stand. I'm intrigued. We sit around a bonfire. A blonde guy named Chris and I start talking. We down beer after beer, until I find myself under his large body on a random sofa. He takes out a condom, enters me and comes after two minutes.

A few minutes pass. "Is everything OK?" he asks.

"Yeah, sure," I reply, avoiding eye contact.

He gets up from the sofa, says "good night" and we each go our own way. The next day at the guesthouse I don't even get a "good morning."

After this painful experience I decide to find a less transient place to stay. I arrive at a meditation center in San Marcus next to Lake Atitlan in Guatemala. The plan is to stay three weeks for a spiritual course but instead I quit the startup and live there for eight months.

In the advanced course, I enter 40 days of silence under the guidance of a Guatemalan teacher and work on nutrition, yoga and lucid dreaming (a process whereby a person becomes conscious and active while dreaming). In these dreams I rediscover my imaginary world as a little girl. Curious, I want to go deeper into the process, to cancel out the background noise: I shave my head, close my Facebook account and postpone my studies for the following year. I discover a new pastime — I sit on the lawn, watching people arriving, and take pictures of them in my mind. A few days later, when their workshop is over, I observe the changes they have undergone: how much warmer they are, how they have taken to smiling and looking others in the eye, how much slower their gait has become. Tears of happiness flow from my eyes.

I feel alive, curious and connected. In my mind the question keeps repeating itself: how do you live with the demands of everyday life, as a contributing member of society, without running off to some mountain? How do you make a living doing what gives you satisfaction? I decide that this will be my life's mission—to initiate projects that will help people live with a similar sense of fulfilment. I want to help others do what the meditation center had done for me — altered my plans and steered me away from the predictable path I was on. I spend most of my time imagining what such a life might look like.

I'M 23. Back from my trip. I team up with a group of people and together we launch a social organization called "This Is It," which promotes cultural initiatives that offer employment opportunities to disadvantaged groups.

To stay focused, I decide to abstain from sex and dating, and concentrate solely on the initiative. I'm totally revved up, passionate, the way I used to feel every time I met someone new. We receive a lot of positive feedback. I appear on stages at international conferences, am interviewed on TV along with my partners, and our organizational model is taught in academic courses focused on social action. My whole life energy is invested in this initiative.

I start studying psychology and film at Tel Aviv University and move into a shared apartment in the city center. Despite all the enthusiasm, I've eaten through my savings and still can't draw a salary. People don't really understand what our organization does and claim that while we make a lot of noise, when it comes down to it, our model is messy and our social impact unclear.

I'M 25 and four projects into my career which have created employment opportunities for people from disadvantaged sectors of society. Still lacking a financial model that can support us, we continue to work as volunteers. I live off the money my grandfather left me, telling myself that he would have been happy to see me spending it this way.

After two years of not being with a man, I reconnect with Alon, whom I've known and liked since elementary school, over an assignment for one of my film classes. I ask for his help as a sound technician. A few meetings later we are a couple, and he becomes the fourth and last man I ever sleep with. As usual, the sex is nothing to write home about, and I usually lie there limply, waiting for it to be over.

I'M 26. We still can't afford to put our staff on salaries and I've spent all of my grandfather's money. What's more, I've fallen into debt and can't pay next month's rent. I have no choice but to move back in with my parents, give up my aspiration to create social change and return to hi-tech. I start participating in women's circles, where, for the first time, I meet women who have fulfilling sex lives, orgasm and all.

One evening, after another frustrating sexual encounter, I make a vow: my body will experience pleasure. Alone or with a partner, pleasure will be part of my life.

THIS BOOK SHARES MY JOURNEY TOWARDS SEXUALITY AND HOW THIS CHANGE IN MY LIFE SAVED MY RELATIONSHIP, INCREASED MY CONFIDENCE AND EVEN INFLUENCED MY CAREER.

While I was working on it, many people asked (some skeptically and others enthusiastically) why a book about sexuality? And won't it come at a personal price?

I'M WRITING FOR THREE MAIN REASONS:
1. **For women who learned how to say no and are now choosing what to say yes to.**

We live in exciting times. As women, we can finally speak up about what we don't want others doing with our bodies, with our rights, with our wages. We can say "no more." But saying no and taking responsibility for our boundaries is only the first step in realizing our potential and power as women.

We must also understand and communicate what we *do* want: we are not here only to survive; we're here to prosper, follow our curiosity and realize our ideas. While supporting the struggle for survivors of sexual abuse, we create a world in which women are no longer victims, a world in which we are also leaders.

If we succeed in changing our perception of our body, we will be able to change our perception of all our roles in society. A woman who realizes that her body's needs in the bedroom are important will also realize that her opinions matter in the conference room and that her ideas are worthy enough to create the resources to make them a reality.

It is time for us women to reclaim our sexuality: to observe it, understand it, heal it — and thereby gain access to our own strength.

2. For women who aren't fulfilling themselves sexually.

Some of us repress, some of us compromise, some of us don't even have a sex life. Deep inside we know that there is something big that we are missing out on. My sexual awakening influenced all aspects of my life — my health, relationships, career, confidence — which is why I believe that sharing this process with other wo.men (women and men) can benefit those who wish to embark on a similar path.

3. To heal the relationship between men and women.

In recent years, the gaps between genders have become evident. There is much anger, confusion, lack of understanding, discrimination, and violence. In my work with individuals and groups, I have discovered processes that support our connection to the body, which are meaningful in the healing process between genders. I have been privileged to witness moments of grace and glimpse a world where men and women can live in harmony. The time has come to make these tools accessible in ways tailored to workplaces, schools, organizations, and the media.

Unfortunately, in the society we live in, the leisure and resources required to participate in workshops within the scope of work or in mind-body processes in personal life are still not accessible to a large part of the population. With humility, I intend to continue contributing my part to change this and make knowledge and tools on these topics accessible to women from all socio-economic backgrounds. If the desire arises to collaborate in creating such spaces, you will find further details at the end of the book.

Part of my personal journey of self-discovery included intense experiences through workshops and therapies, but each person has their own suitable path. Nowadays, when asked if I recommend participating in similar workshops to the ones I have attended, I say that I do not have the audacity to recommend what is suitable for another person and that it is important to be aware of the risks involved. In our exploration of the body, we must proceed with curiosity and sensitivity: an inappropriate workshop or treatment with an unsuitable person can cause psychological harm. Sexual workshops do not replace trauma therapy or individual therapeutic support from professionals. Each one of us comes with a different background, and intense experiences, like all intense experiences in life, can also trigger post-traumatic expectations. As we have learned from stories in recent years, intimate situations in such workshops can become platforms for attackers to commit sexual abuse. Therefore, no matter which path you choose in exploring the body, remember to be sensitive and attentive to what suits you and choose a safe environment that meets your needs. There are numerous ways to connect with the body, and there is an abundance of information available today on the internet. This book describes just one journey among infinite journeys that can be taken on the path to connecting with the body.

CONTEXT / SHORT BIO

In sharing this story, Alon and I have chosen to relinquish some of our privacy in order to share the journey and inspire individual paths that suit each person. Present Woman can encourage embarking on a journey of getting acquainted with the body and exploring sexuality, and enable this path to illuminate and awaken life.

In response to numerous inquiries from readers, this book also includes a complementary journey that allows experimentation with tools and documenting the exploration. It can be reached through the attached link.

www.narkisalon.com/booklet-en

CHAPTER 1
SO THIS IS WHAT AN ORGASM FEELS LIKE?

"Woman... such an interesting creature"
Golda Meir

It took me years to believe I was worthy of being with a good person. Alon is pure-hearted and non-judgmental. When someone asks him for help, he doesn't think twice before coming to their aid. He is totally authentic, sometimes in ways that catch me off guard, and doesn't stand on ceremony. I met him in elementary school when I was ten; even back then we liked each other. Thirteen years later, we became a couple.

Alon studied accounting. The Excel documents he created were works of art. He devised financial forecasts not only for well-funded projects, but for any project that sought his assistance, often on a pro bono basis. Patiently, he would guide his clients through the process of creating year-long forecasts—the first step towards turning their bold ideas into reality.

After a year into the relationship, I moved in with Alon, to his parents basement. It would be six months before we could afford a place of our own. Every few weeks I'd come up with an idea for a new project—a fund that invests in schools for entrepreneurs; a media company that produces consciousness-raising films; a company that offers teambuilding workshops for hi-tech firms. Every idea entailed countless hours of conversation with potential partners, in addition to creating presentations and documents to present to investors. All this I would do on Skype or from the phone in our basement abode. Then came time for Alon's Excel, whose handiwork would do even a company on NASDAQ proud.

Alon was the first partner I had who was as warm as me. For the first time in my life I wasn't made to feel that I was overdoing it with my hugs. We would hug for hours. The place I planted the most kisses was his neck, and my head found a home on his right shoulder.

After four months together, I went on vacation in London and sent him a text: "I love you." He didn't reply. When I got back he explained that the text had stressed him out. Putting my hand on his, I said: "I don't need you to say it back. I know you love me. I can feel it." A few days later he said it back.

We fantasized about the future: we'd live in a village, or on some mountain with friends, working the land together. We'd binge-watch TV, participate in yoga workshops, walk barefoot around the Ramat Aviv mall and giggle at the sight of all the suburban moms staring at our bare feet.

Alon was a great cook, and I a great cheerleader from a safe distance away. We would give each other massages for hours, cry together, laugh together, and make the most of every moment together. What we liked doing most was making music— improvising new songs, singing covers and dreaming about a joint performance and an album.

My relationship with Alon came with some heavy sexual baggage. Sex was painful for me, both physically and emotionally.

And the fact that I often didn't know what moves to make—and that the moves I did make left me feeling frozen and fake—didn't help matters. From this place, I came to avoid sexual activity as much as possible. But the love between Alon and me was so deep that it compensated for this deficiency, and at one point our relationship almost became asexual, as if we were siblings or friends without benefits.

At the start of our relationship, I did what I always did in bed: pretend I was having a good time, that I was on top of things (even when I was on the bottom), and that I was reaching some small satisfaction. But the truth was that intercourse was often painful. Alon and I would lie in bed, embracing, and I would move from kissing his neck to licking his ear and hugging him tight. My expressions of warmth and affection turned Alon on. At first, he would hug me back and kiss me in the same way, but soon he was ready for action. The faster his pace, the slower I was to respond; on the outside I was a willing partner in the game I was so practiced in, putting on the "right" face and even making the right sounds. A few moments later he would say, "I'll get a condom," and I would wait in bed, frozen like a statue.

I hated the feeling of rubber inside me, but I wasn't on the pill, so I didn't really have a choice. Going for penetration, Alon would encourage me to relax, while stroking and kissing me. As he moved back and forth, I'd try to ease into his rhythm, but I was so tense, and time wasn't on my side. Before I knew it, Alon would raise his head slightly upwards, open his eyes, gasp and then, boom, it was all over.

That was more or less what our ritual was like.

My friends used to openly speak about sex, but something about the way they spoke seemed insincere. There were the "nymphos," who found the act easy and fun, who initiated sex more than their partners and "fucked" their men, rather than the other way around. These women seemed nothing less than invulnerable. One would speak about how her man went down on her, another she felt like sitting on his face, or spent hours fucking the day before, as if it was as simple and as natural as drinking tea. Others didn't talk about it at all, **but gave the impression that everything was fine and so what was there to talk about?**

I felt damaged in that group, so I kept what was going on between Alon and me to myself. I continued trying to make love with this man I loved so much, but mainly waited for it to be over so we could go on hugging.

IN THE MEANTIME, THE OVERDRAFT IN MY BANK ACCOUNT told me it was time to find new ways to make a living. I decided that if I was going to set out on an entrepreneurial path again, this time it would be for pay. A friend told me about a project that offered professional training for start-up jobs and introduced me to Avi, the entrepreneur in charge of fundraising. There was an instant click. My experience in building a local brand with a social organization, combined with my sale skills, were just what the project needed.

"Ultimately," said Avi, "our success will be determined by our ability to sell these courses to students."

We got down to work. Two months later, I deposited my first paycheck and had the space to breathe again. I was excited to enter this new world of content, and by the opportunity to start a business with people who had real business experience.

When I re-entered the start-up world, it was at the height of its hype, and those who made it, made it big. These entrepreneurs were considered heroes who would lead the world in a better direction, towards progress. The notion was that in order to solve wide-scale problems you had to function like a start-up.

I remember reading about large fundraising campaigns led by companies like Uber and WeWork and realizing they weren't even turning a profit. I was shocked. Why were investors continuing to fund them, while we fought over every penny, making sure we didn't incur any losses? Later I learned why: These companies had a vision for the future, a vision that was potentially very profitable. As long as a company managed to show growth, the investors believed that it might one day offer the solution for a massive global need—which would translate to huge profits that would justify the investments made to build the company. For this reason, every startup wanted to be the winner in its market, to hit the jackpot, and everyone knew that speed was the name of the game. Myself included.

Beyond trying to make money, our business also addressed the less privileged sectors of society, which I felt offered a chance for significant social change. My previous path, comprised of small social entrepreneurial projects, had not brought me the fulfillment I was seeking. Not only did the projects reach only a limited number of people, they also came with paltry pay. I wanted to understand this new system, where everything was based on data, and investors and target goals motivated people to move faster to the finish line. I thrive on competition, especially when my competitors are lions.

AVI AND I BRANDED THE TRAINING CENTER AS AN ACADEMY and started marketing the courses we had created with companies and well-known lecturers in the hi-tech industry. My job was to interview people in the field and try to understand what additional professions we could help make available to our students as a result of the training we offered. Every person I met was more interesting than the previous one. They were all super smart and spoke at an even faster clip than I did about topics I knew nothing about. My intellect was challenged in a way it hadn't been in the world of social initiative. It reminded me of how my father used to challenge us at home. My father is one of the greatest mathematicians in the world; when talking to him, no matter what the topic was, I always felt, even as a child, that I had to choose my words carefully and come to every conversation at least partially prepared. I couldn't say things that were unfounded or that I didn't fully understand just because they might be right.

In the startup world I came across many figures who evoked that same sense of awe in me. I remember the first time I encountered Paul Graham's blog. Paul is the founder of an accelerator named **Y Combinator**, a program that invested small sums of money in projects at very early stages of development, quickly procuring exposure for investors, mentors and knowledge so that ideas could be translated into action as quickly as possible. Y Combinator was considered the best accelerator in the world, with Dropbox, Airbnb and Stripe among the companies it supported. I fantasized about being accepted to the program, living in San Francisco, attending official dinners as one of the only women present, gaining knowledge, networking and building a knock-'em-dead startup. To me, Paul Graham was everything that was new and thought-worthy in the world. I viewed him as a contemporary Aristotle. The same world I had escaped a few years earlier, on my post-army trip, had come to embody everything I wanted to excel at.

One of the best places to acquire all these skills was at the Board of Directors' meetings with our investors. At these meetings they would talk about a hundred thousand dollars in the same way I would about twenty. They knew every start-up worth knowing and were in contact with investors from across the globe. I lapped up every last detail, determined to show that I was giving this job my all..

It was challenging at first: they tossed around a lot of terms I wasn't familiar with when referring to a company's worth, fundraising, and distribution of stocks to employees. During those initial meetings, my ideas and feelings would often be written off as "fluff" ;for instance, I would say: "I think that in this workshop we should have thirty people. If we have any more it won't allow for a meaningful experience."

And they would say: "That's a fluff argument. The question is how much the classroom costs, how much each one of them is paying you, how much the lecturers cost, what percentage of profit you assume you'll reach in your business plan — this is how you determine your price. And if the price doesn't allow you to create an experience that will cause the students to come back, then go find a product that will. Otherwise, it's of no interest."

When I saw that arguing didn't lead anywhere, I changed course. After poring over the Excel document, I'd prepare answers to all the questions that might arise so that I could support my gut feelings with logical arguments.

Namedropping was a key strategy I used to compensate for my knowledge gap. For example, I'd mention the name of the father of someone I had studied with who was now managing an investment fund, or talk about how much money the people related to him had. I'd talk about a friend of my parents who sold a company to Microsoft, or another friend who worked for Google and could help with grants for new projects. I remember the day I became fluent in their language. Someone was talking about WeWork, about their faulty business model, and I jumped up and said: "They just raised 5 billion dollars, they've got enough time to come up with a better one." Two of the men exchanged smiles and looked at me proudly[1].

A YEAR AFTER ESTABLISHING THE COMPANY, Avi and I hired our first full-time

---

[1] This conversation took place during WeWork's euphoric era. Five years later, when the company released its data forecasts, the inflated estimations were exposed.

employee to handle marketing. Avital was five years older than me. We scheduled our first training session at 8:30 A.M.. At 8:40 she sent me a WhatsApp: "I'll be there at around 9:00. I had a breastfeeding issue." I was shocked. I was furious.

At 9:00 she stepped in and sat down across from me.

"I expect you to be here on time," I said, "and certainly not to update me at the last minute by text."

She was taken aback. "I had a breastfeeding issue..." she reminded me.

"So start breastfeeding earlier, just like I organize things ahead of time to get here on time," I said.

The meeting was tense. Later I called a friend who also ran a startup to tell him what had happened. Siding with me, he said: "Breastfeeding is no excuse. Just like pregnancy isn't a sickness. If women want equality they better stop using things like that as excuses."

"So true," I agreed.

A few months later we hired more employees. We had two additional young mothers in the company, who often needed us to show consideration: when their child got sick, had adjustment issues at daycare, didn't sleep at night, etc.

One day, I joined a morning meeting with other female hi-tech entrepreneurs. The idea was to discuss the various challenges we faced and offer each other advice. I was first teamed up with Shira, a well-known CEO in the industry, who led a startup that had more than fifty employees, with branches in New York, San Francisco and Tel Aviv. For the next fifteen minutes, we talked about the issues that mothers of young children often brought to the workplace.

"I know what you mean," Shira nodded. "When my working moms complain about the challenges of balancing family and career, I explain that they should appreciate the fact they can leave early twice a week and work at night from home. If they still complain," she added with a smile, "just say: 'You wanna handle it differently? Go, raise money, open your own business and do it your way, but don't expect to reach a better family-career balance when you're the entrepreneur — that's when things really get hard." We both giggled in mutual understanding, her hand met mine, we hi-fived and moved on to the next round.

ONE DAY, GOOGLE CALLED FOR PROPOSALS to help advance women in hi-tech. At the time I had no plans to focus on women as a target audience, but who wouldn't want to work with Google? We filled out the form and designed a course for our academy that would allow women to produce business projects and evaluate them in a way suited to their own needs. We combined the usual business methodologies with mind-body content: yoga, meditation, emotional sharing and time in the desert without cell phones. To our surprise, our suggestion was accepted. Our idea was chosen to be one of forty trial programs that Google would fund worldwide to support women.

I invited Sarah, one of my best friends and someone who had already given many mind-body workshops, to lead the program with me. To understand who Sarah is, you have to see her in action. For example, one day I met her at a café, where she was holding a rabbit in her lap.

"What's that?" I asked.

"I took it from the kindergarten next door," she replied, stroking the bunny. "It hurt its eye and needs eye drops every two hours."

Sarah also treated people who suffered from PTSD. One of her patients had scars all over his face. She'd sometimes hug him for fifteen minutes straight, because she was the only woman who could do so sincerely without feeling repulsed.

The first workshop took place with 27 female entrepreneurs from seven different countries. Some of their projects were at the idea phase, some were underway, and some needed to renew their energy reserves to continue working.

At the start of the workshop, all cell phones were handed over to make way for the desert's stillness. This together time devoted to thinking about their projects helped these women mine their inner strength: They worked on their business model, planned a pilot for new products, exchanged fundraising pitches and worked on skills such as time management and presentations.

And one more thing: since it was only women and we were practicing mind-body exercises, a new emotional layer was revealed. For example, one evening as we sat in the Bedouin tent before dinner, we started asking each other questions: "What's the scariest moment you've ever experienced?" "What are your dreams?" "Regrets?" Some women shared stories about rape and harassment, others about feeling body shame in the workplace, and still others about hidden desires they didn't dare communicate, even to their partners.

The next morning, we went on a silent walk, where I saw some of the women who had only met the day before holding hands, like little girls.

At the concluding session I was moved to tears. The group reminded me of that reassuring female figure who used to visit me in my childhood daydreams. During the workshop I was reminded that being a woman meant something, that we derive our power from different sources, and that there were things in my life that I was still missing.

After the workshop, we continued meeting once a month to work on our projects and share profound events from our lives; the women who didn't live in Israel joined us on Skype.

For the first time, I witnessed a vulnerable and candid discourse between women. I learned the true meaning of the word "complex" and even though we had come together to talk about careers, many of us gravitated to the subject of our sex lives. After reintroducing the subject with my friends, it turned out they were no different, even those who had presented a rosy picture. They all reported first-hand feelings of repression, shame, darkness and an abiding need to please.

Many of the women I spoke to admitted that they didn't enjoy penetration. They said things like: "It's OK, but most of the time I just wait for it to be over"; "He cowers over me like an animal and I pretend to groan." These were all strong women on the outside who, when it came to sex, compensated by keeping quiet, like a debt that had to be paid in order to keep the relationship going. Until we confided in each other, we hadn't even realized there were issues that bothered us, or that there might be another way.

Of course there were also women who enjoyed penetration, but some said they took more pleasure in other things, like receiving oral sex, or their guy focusing on their G-spot or playing with their clitoris. Many women hadn't ever experienced an orgasm during sex but spoke instead of specific enjoyment. And there were a few rare, most intriguing women, who shared that they were trying to reach something powerful with their partners that would bring them to a new height of pleasure—it was actually a joint mission of theirs. Suddenly, I was hearing about women who were the focus of the sexual encounter, with partners who would sometimes spend even an entire hour just on them. I never knew anything like that existed, much less considered it a possibility.

The more women I spoke to, the more I yearned for a change in my own situation. The community of female entrepreneurs we had formed met each one of us where we were: it gave some a push to ask for a raise, others the courage to start a fundraising campaign, or to demand to be listened to in boardroom meetings. For me it did something life-changing: made me understand that it was time to start focusing on my needs, including in the bedroom.

I ALMOST NEVER CLIMAXED WITH A PARTNER. When I was by myself I could come in a cinch, but with a partner it took me forever and I didn't really know how to guide Alon.

At the start of our relationship Alon would spend a long time trying, but since it didn't yield results it embarrassed me. I would steer him away from my vagina and we would concentrate on him. That dynamic became our habit in the bedroom: I'd pretend I was enjoying myself and then move on to pleasing him. It was a cinch to make Alon come.

Taking inspiration from the women's circles, I shared my feelings with Alon and suggested that from now on we dedicate time to helping me come. The task wasn't as simple as I thought it would be. Once in a long while something worked and I felt pleasure, but most of the time I was frozen. I tried giving him instructions: "Too strong, too slow, too fast. That doesn't feel good," until at one point I became paralyzed and said, "I don't want to continue, pull out."

Now Alon was the frozen one. His confidence dropped and he felt that no matter what he did or how he touched me, I wasn't satisfied. But from my point of view, it was a corrective to years of keeping quiet and focusing on the other's needs.

Those days most of our sexual encounters would end like this: I'd stop in the middle with, "This doesn't feel good,"; Alon would turn his back to me, I would turn my back to him, and we would remain silent for a long time. On top of that, all my instructions and abruptness led to a situation in which Alon also almost never came. Every time it failed, I felt a surge of frustration, which made me even less attentive: the last thing I was in the mood for was concentrating on Alon's needs.

Alon said he thought I was doing it on purpose, which turned my frustration into anger: "The world has been carrying on as usual for years without my orgasm, so why can't it carry on without yours?"

"It's not the same thing. I have to work really hard to make you come," he tried to reason, which made matters only worse.

The truth is, I was also angry about things that were beyond Alon's control: years of neglecting my own needs, and especially those of my body. When I was younger, instead of discovering my sexual likes and dislikes, I was busy learning the moves and sounds that my partner expected of me. We led a double life as a couple: we had a beautiful and deep bond of love and friendship, and at the same time, whenever we were in bed, we were at a loss.

MY SEXUAL FRUSTRATION STARTED SPILLING OVER TO MY WORK. Every morning I'd walk into the office at WeWork. The receptionists would smile at me and say, "Good morning, Narkis," and then go back to their phones, a neon sign above them reading, "Work hard, play harder."

I would pour myself a cup of tea, then go into our little office clad with cluttered desks and chairs that served our six alternating employees. At 9:30 I'd turn on my computer. Dozens of emails waited in my inbox, and I tried to answer all of them. From 10:00 to 1:00 I'd make sales calls to persuade as many students as possible to enroll in our courses. In between calls, people on my team would come to me with questions and problems. I would pour myself more and more tea so that eventually I'd be forced to take a break—if only to the bathroom.

At 1:00 I'd order something from one of the food kiosks outside, and swallow it down while staring at my screen. After lunch, meetings: with my team and course lecturers and companies we were collaborating with on placements or joint courses.

The community of women Sarah and I had established as a side project within the business that Avi and I were running was still functioning, but I no longer had the energy to invest in it, and Sarah and I weren't getting along as well as we had initially. The more confronted I was by the kind of thinking that measured everything in numbers, the more difficult it was for us to work together. While Sarah raised ideas, I listened and cringed, imagining having to explain these expenses to management.

I'd stop her in the middle and ask, "But how are we going to finance this? What's the business model?"

"Not everything has to cost money," she replied. "We can publish content on Facebook and then more women will want to join us, so it would be like marketing." "But who's going to do it? We don't have time, we've got to fill up the next workshop and I'm busy with other things. It sounds nice, but it's fluff."

She couldn't understand my reaction at first, but one day she burst out, "You dismiss every idea I have! It doesn't seem like you actually want to continue helping these women. Maybe you're not interested in this project any longer."

Sarah took a step back and stopped scheduling meetings with me. At this point, I started asking myself questions about my work. Of course, I couldn't devise systems of support for other women in their jobs or help with any of the other topics Sarah had mentioned, because I was feeling awful about myself. How could I teach women anything? I didn't even know how to have sex.

AT THE SAME TIME, Shahar, a good friend of ours, came back from a two-week Tantra workshop. I had no clue what that meant, but I knew it was something sexual and I felt the change in energy he transmitted. He was joyful, his body seemed relaxed, and his spirits were high. Shahar wasn't someone who had moved to live on a hilltop in India. He was like me, part of the rat race. He had been working in the restaurant industry and was preparing for an MBA abroad. If he saw the light, maybe I could too.

"What goes on at those Tantra workshops? How come you suddenly look like you're on top of the world?" I asked him.

Shahar grinned. "It's like a sexuality workshop. You have to experience it to understand," he said.

"Come on... tell me more," I pressed on.

"Basically, it's about learning to work with your sexual energy. It touches on every aspect of life, even things that don't seem related to sexuality are influenced by it."

"I've got to learn this," I decided right then and there. "But how? I won't travel alone and Alon and I can barely have sex without fighting."

"You could have a private session instead of a workshop," Shahar suggested. "I'll get you in touch with Rachel, she's a sex therapist."

I had nothing to lose. I needed a change, pronto. I told Alon about it. He was as clueless as I was but encouraged me to give it a try. Our problems weren't going anywhere—and weren't going to solve themselves.

HOW DO YOU PREPARE FOR A SEXUAL THERAPY SESSION? 10 a.m. Our apartment was empty. In my room stood a table, two chairs, an armchair and a bed. I wiped down the chairs, changed the sheets and fluffed the pillows. I showered and put on a green dress. Impatient, I constantly checked the time. Suddenly, the doorbell rang. I opened the door and a young Asian woman, about five feet tall, crossed the threshold.

"Hi, I'm Rachel," she said with a foreign accent and extended her hand. It was gentle and warm, as were her expression and energy.

We went into my room, where a small table with tea and plate of dried fruit awaited us. I was so embarrassed that I dove right into both.

"Tell me what brings you to our meeting," she began when we sat down.

I shifted uncomfortably in my chair. It was actually the first time I had spoken to a stranger about our sexual problems. "I've never managed to enjoy sex," I said. "There are some nice moments, occasionally even pleasurable ones, but it's nothing like what my friends describe. Until now, I've always pretended with partners, but I'm in a loving relationship now, and it's the first time that I'm confronting the issue and communicating everything that is missing for me in sex."

"So what are you missing?" Rachel asked without a hint of criticism in her voice.

"I don't climax. I need a lot of time, or to be touched in a specific way. I'm not sure. And I don't want to continue faking orgasms. I raised the subject with Alon, but things haven't improved. On the contrary, it's creating a lot of tension and has brought us to a dead end. I feel as if there might be something wrong with me."

Rachel listened patiently, nodding after each sentence.

"Many women experience what you're describing," she assured me.

"Yes, I know, but that doesn't make me feel better. Ever since I told him how I feel, he's just even more discouraged. I've taken away all his confidence in sex with me. Now we're both frustrated. I feel distant from my body. I have no idea how to fix this. I thought that a session with you might help."

"Women are often frustrated by how their partners touch them, but they themselves don't know what they like, and they don't take the time to find out," Rachel said. "So how can they expect someone else to know? Our *Yoni* is intuitive and wise. She opens only if there is sincere, deep intention. You have to treat her very gently and learn her rhythm. Our Yoni is like a temple, you have to ask permission to enter and hear the reply from inside."

"What's a Yoni?"

"Oh, sorry," Rachel giggled. "The Yoni is the female sexual organ, the vulva, in Sanskrit."

"Cool. What's the penis called?"

"Lingam."

"Sounds good. I'll use it."

I took two last sips of tea, which had long since gone cold, and said, "I've never talked to my Yoni. I have no idea how to ask things of her and definitely no idea how to listen to her."

Rachel gave me an empathetic smile and then said with her gentle voice, "What we'll do in this session is a massage. I won't speak and I suggest that you don't either, unless there is something important you want to tell me. The goal of the massage is that you listen and connect to the way your body feels and then connect to your Yoni and sexuality. I'm here to support your process. Don't pay attention to me. The best thing would be if you could forget that I was even here and concentrate on your inner core."

I had no idea what she meant or what she was going to do, but I felt safe. For some reason, I completely trusted her.

"OK," I said, "what do I do?"

"Take your clothes off," said Rachel.

"Should I leave my underpants on?"

"If you like."

My heart started pounding. No one was home, but I locked the door just in case. I knew that I was about to have an experience that would change my life, and hopefully for the better, but I was also worried that I was doing something that was wrong or forbidden.

For the first time, I was about to engage in something sexual with a person who was:

a. A woman.

b. Sexual professional.

c. Not my partner.

Would I "get caught," and then be jailed or burned at the stake?

I LAY FACE DOWN, NAKED, ON THE BED with a sheet over me. The main light was off and only the bedside table lamp on. Soft music was playing. Rachel started by pressing my back, followed by my legs and hands. Then she asked me to roll over and she massaged my feet. I love massages, it's my favorite thing in the whole world. The longer she massaged me, the more relaxed I became. I let go of my thoughts, as if I'd forgotten about Rachel's existence and the reason she had come.

At one point she stopped and asked quietly: "Can I touch your Yoni?"

Would it be cheating? I asked myself and immediately replied to myself that I was sure Alon wouldn't mind. Rachel's presence was so delicate, I felt as if her fingers were my fingers, and that I was alone with myself. She touched me in the most respectful and precise way I'd ever been touched. It felt so unspeakably good.

"Yes," I replied, my eyes still shut.

As Rachel placed her finger on my Yoni, I felt the whole of me opening up and melting on the inside. I didn't think of her as the source of these sensations, I felt like it was something that my body was allowing itself.

A few minutes later she stopped and asked in that quiet way of hers: "Can I enter your Yoni?" Until that point she had only touched the external parts.

"Yes," I replied without thinking twice.

With her finger, Rachel entered my Yoni and immediately came into contact with my G-spot. A few seconds later the sensation was so powerful that my consciousness left my body. It was like what people describe when they take drugs: the room was spinning around me and I saw colorful shades in the corners of my eyes. The Yoni became wetter and wetter, inviting the finger to enter deeper and deeper. It was all-encompassing; the more my Yoni expanded, the more my heart expanded, along with my perspective, vocal cords and stomach. My whole being became this pulse that invited life to pass through it. I felt as if I was part of everything that *is*. So this was what an orgasm was all about!

I had lost all sense of time. And then Rachel asked, "Can I leave your Yoni?"

"Yes," I replied, even though I didn't want the moment to be over. She took her finger out, placed her hand on my Yoni, looked into my eyes and said: "Now close your eyes and rest. It's time for integration."

I shut my eyes and couldn't stop smiling.

That evening I had dinner with my family. My older sister Nilli saw me enter and immediately asked: "Where have you been? You're glowing."

I smiled but with all the others around, didn't say a word. When dinner was over, I took my sister aside and whispered: "I had my first real orgasm today. I never knew this is how it could feel. I had a sexual therapy session with an amazing woman named Rachel. My whole body is on fire."

Without a beat, my sister asked for Rachel's number.

ALON IMMEDIATELY SAW HOW HAPPY I WAS, and agreed to a joint session.

Rachel asked us what each of us was bringing to the session. Alon wanted us to learn how to have sex in a way that would allow us both to come, and I wanted the exact opposite. My goal was to reach a situation in which Alon could enjoy a sexual encounter with neither of us climaxing. I was hoping our sex life would gain some flexibility if orgasm wasn't in the center of it. Rachel suggested that since I had already had one session, the second one would focus on Alon's body instead of mine.

"I can teach you how to enjoy sex without coming," she promised him.

She guided me through an exercise in which I turned Alon on, gently touching his Lingam and around it in a tickling motion; when his sexual energy rose, she instructed him to distribute it throughout his body without ejaculating. Alon had to breathe at a prescribed pace and imagine his energy rising before it coursed through his body, giving him a life-force. We practiced it a few more times, Alon altering the rhythm of his breathing each time. Rachel asked him to imagine the non-ejaculated energy filling him with strength.

When the session was over the three of us sat on the bed for a postmortem. Alon was reserved, saying only that it was an interesting experience. Rachel encouraged us to continue working on the exercises and promised that at one point things would start flowing naturally. After she left, we continued sitting on the bed with nothing but our underpants on and at our usual loss. We were quiet for a long while until I broke the silence.

"What do you think?" I asked the question I always asked Alon when I didn't know what to say.

"I don't know what I think," he replied.

"What do you feel?"

"I don't know what the whole point was," he said, got up and started to get dressed.

"You're not happy?"

"No, I'm not happy."

"Why?"

"Because I like coming. It's relaxing, and helps me unwind. Why are you making it sound as if it's something bad? Why is my homework to not come? What about the work you need to do? After all, we've reached this point because of your issues."

It doesn't happen often, but I had nothing to say at that moment. I got up from the bed and hugged him. He didn't hug me back.

"It'll be OK. It's a process," I said.

A few days later Rachel returned to Bali and we were left to cope alone. The session had only reinforced Alon's belief that what we needed was something internal, not external. He wouldn't hear of more therapists, workshops or any type of process. He believed that we should keep trying to have sex and that at one point I'd let go and stop feeling stuck. He thought our problems were private and that it wasn't right to share them with others. I didn't know what to think. I felt awful. It had taken so much of my strength to get him to try out this therapy, and the light at the end of the tunnel had grown dark again. We were left to our dysfunctional sex and I was doomed to a life without pleasure.

To compartmentalize, I dove headfirst into the startup that I was leading, dedicating myself from morning to night to one thing, and one thing only: making money.

EVEN THOUGH WE HAD ALL JOINED THE COMPANY to help people make a living doing what they loved, this was not the basis upon which we were evaluated. Since we were a business that relied on shareholders, success meant maximizing profit, and nothing more.

The attitude towards money in the startup world was completely different from what I knew in the social world, where we invested huge efforts in raising donations and finding sponsors. In the startup world it felt as if there were resources everywhere — investments, sponsorships and even government grants.

The feeling was that no matter how much money the startup had — it could always have more. When it was time for another funding round, we sat with a consultant, who looked at our business plan and advised us to write that we intended to open branches in two more countries and increase our enrollment to 3,000 students.

"How are we going to have ten times more students in one year? And why expand abroad? We haven't even begun to realize our full potential here in Israel," I asked.

"With more money you'll be able to do much more than you can imagine right now. You need to show investors that you have growth potential. Israel is a small country. It's enough for you to open one course in another country and call it a branch," he said.

"Maybe I'm missing something, but it doesn't make sense to me."

I hailed from the small and poor world of social initiative. My previous project had a direct impact on no more than a few hundred people annually, and each year we aspired to fundraise no more than the sum required to execute our immediate plans. I simply couldn't adapt to the way of thinking the consultant was trying to instill in me.

That year I appeared on Forbes' Israeli list of the 30 most promising young business people. Looking at my picture, at the smile on my face, the suit I was wearing, my coiffed hair, the description of what I did, I felt light years away from that person. I was presented as a young woman guiding other women to self-fulfillment, but the truth was that I didn't enjoy my work, couldn't understand the economic system that was supposed to be my stomping ground and, worst of all, I had no sex life. I was living a lie.

CHAPTER 2
GATES OPENING

"The truth will set you free, but first it will piss you off!"
Gloria Steinem

THAT YEAR, WHEN THE HOLE IN OUR RELATIONSHIP WAS BECOMING VISIBLE TO US, we decided to get married. The decision might have come from desperation, or a need for distraction, or the feeling that our relationship required a shift that would offer deliverance; or maybe it came from the great love and friendship that existed between us. We both wanted to believe in a happy ending, and that it might lie just around the corner of the wedding canopy...

Being in bed together led us back into that familiar loop of despondent sex, frustration and fighting. I tried to avoid intimacy as much as possible. I'd stay at the office until 7, then talk with my partner Avi on the drive home about how the day went and what tasks still needed doing. Our conversations always dragged on and I'd often sit in the parked car outside our apartment for an extra forty minutes. Then I'd walk in exhausted, give Alon a split-second hug, and break out my phone or turn on the TV.

At some point, Alon would join me in bed. We hardly ever touched each other anymore. We had become more like roommates: good friends who talk about their day and occasionally laugh at a mutual joke. Most of the time we were in avoidance mode, with Alon maintaining his refusal to try either a workshop or therapy.

Until one day, after yet another post-sex fight, I wouldn't have it anymore. It was one of those moments of enlightenment in which you say to yourself: this can't be my life — this is not what I came here for. I realized that as long as this sexual stagnation persisted, I was doomed to forever feel insecure, insincere, and suffer from FOMO—Fear of Missing Out. If I didn't stand up for myself now, it might soon be too late.

Inspired by these insights, I did the unthinkable — imposed an ultimatum: "Either we start sexual therapy or I won't have sex with you anymore."

An angry Alon turned his back to me. But this time, instead of doing the same, I did something different.

"My love," I said, choking up, "I feel completely lost. We need help — it's our only chance. For the sake of our relationship, of the life we deserve to live, please, please join me on this journey."

Alon turned to me, wiped away my tears and took me in his arms.

OUR FRIEND SHAHAR RECOMMENDED A THERAPIST NAMED SANAND. I texted Sanand, who wrote back with a few words about the process and herself: "There is great strength in our sexuality. Our sexuality is sacred and healing. My commitment as a therapist is to support you through this wondrous journey you have chosen, to accompany you and offer you tools that will help you realize your goal and be available for questions surrounding the difficulties that arise along the way. In our meetings we will learn how to breathe, move, free ourselves of inhibitions, listen to sensations. We will learn to touch and re-experience touch, recognize restricting patterns, open up the body's armor. Every session is personally adapted to the unique needs you come with! Please write clearly and honestly — what are your expectations of this process? What do you want to focus on?"

On this, Alon and I were of one mind: Healing. The word came out of our mouths at the same moment.

Sanand lives in Rosh Pina, a ways away, so on top of the charged emotional atmosphere between Alon and me, the journey began with a long drive along dark narrow roads. Alon sat at the wheel and we listened to music on the radio in silence.

An hour and forty minutes later, we arrived. We parked on the street, found the house, opened the green gate and walked up the stairs to the clinic.

Sanand's clinic was an embracing space: a room that reminded me of a womb, half-dark half-light, a purple wall-to-wall carpet and the smell of incense. Sanand greeted us. Barefoot, in a burgundy dress and a long beaded chain around her neck, she looked like she was in her fifties. She was gorgeous, with fair eyes, blonde curly hair and a wide smile that conveyed wisdom and love. Just stepping into the room took the edge off after the tense drive.

"What brought you to me?" she asked.

I told her point-blank, as I had told Rachel, about my struggle with the need to please during sex, that it was hard to respond to my partner's needs without addressing my own, and that I couldn't climax. But this time Alon was there right next to me and I couldn't stop crying while talking.

When it was Alon's turn to speak he said, "We've been in the same loop for a long time. I'd rather not add to this story. We've come here to create a new one."

Sanand smiled. "OK, so let's leave the story and go straight to the body," she suggested.

Sanand's first exercise started with listening to our breathing, followed by contracting our sexual organ with the inhale and releasing on the exhale. We were clothed and the experience was personal. It was a little hard at first, but once I got into the rhythm I felt sexual stimulation and a sense of vitality throughout my body.

Then she asked us to look into each other's eyes; gradually, the distance that had grown between us over the past few months began to dissolve.

In the next exercise, we told one another how we wanted to have our hand touched and the other had to repeat in words what they understood. If there was anything that needed correcting, we would correct it and try again until we got it right. Then we switched. The exercise exemplified the importance of communication and what it can yield when one dedicates oneself to pleasure another.

Another exercise included Alon sitting with his legs crossed and me sitting on his lap with my legs spread, facing him. With open mouths, we pressed our lips together and synchronized our breathing. When Alon breathed out I breathed in, and vice versa. Our breathing soon synchronized, and it felt as if we had become one body. Alon was completely into it. I could tell it was turning him on and it also started doing something for me. The intensity of the energy that moved between us was hard to contain and I wanted to stop, even though I was being swept away. This was often what happened to me during sex—when something became too intense, I sought an escape route.

I continued with the exercise and looked at Alon, who was really giving it his all. For a moment I could see us from the side, fighting for our relationship and our sex life, listening to this woman, who a moment ago had been a complete stranger, and faithfully following her every word. Detaching my lips from his, I gazed into his eyes, like in the previous exercise, but this time without being instructed. How I loved this man, was all I could think of.

Alon gazed back at me, equally moved. Picking up on that vibe, Sanand instructed us to stand and touch each other's hearts. Alon placed his hand on my heart and then on his own. Suddenly he burst into tears.

"I just saw the whole essence of our relationship," Alon said to Sanand and me. "I feel as if we really are holding each other's hearts."

This heart connection built a new trust between us, which became the basis for dismantling some of the obstacles in the following sessions with Sanand. This was the first time I had experienced the resolution of deep conflict through body work. Through our bodies we acquired tools for communication that helped guide us in our sexual encounters.

Sanand imparted this invaluable insight: The hardest thing for women is to surrender themselves, and the hardest thing for men is not to be selfish.

"Every time you feel blocked," she added, "Use these magic words. You say to her: 'I'm here for you,' and you reply: 'I trust you'."

In the next session, we continued using our bodies to communicate, and in the third and fourth sessions we moved on to more intimate touching.

We started with Alon, who explained what things gave him pleasure in bed, what his needs were during sex and what bothered him. Sanand didn't think it was necessary for Alon to focus on not climaxing.

"There's nothing wrong with climaxing," she said. "The only problem is being dependent on it. You need to approach the sexual encounter without an agenda, and whatever it yields, it yields."

In the fourth session we focused on my Yoni. Alon tried what Rachel had done with me, which released a lot of emotional pain. Sanand's instructions focused on pace and how to communicate. I could see that she saw how hard it was for me to have my Yoni touched by Alon. At the end of that session she told us we had made wonderful progress, and suggested that I come by myself to the next sessions.

"It seems as if there's something deeper you need to address in your sexuality; before you bring Alon into the story, you should try confronting it alone," she said.

ALON WAS PLEASED. Even though he appreciated the process with Sanand, the drives back and forth took a toll on him, and at one point he reached his limit. I accepted her offer because I knew there was something unresolved in me that required attention. The sense of being stuck and absent during sex had happened with every partner I ever had, and if Sanand could help me work on that, both I and my relationship with Alon would benefit.

After our first one-on-one session, Sanand said: "You have the symptoms of someone who has experienced sexual abuse. Your body is tight and rejects touch. It interprets every touch as painful or ticklish. You are excessively sensitive to tickling, which suggests an energy blockage." I knew there was something to what she was saying. Ever since I could remember, I didn't feel safe with men, but I could never identify the source of that discomfort. I wanted to connect with my body and heal it.

In our private sessions, Sanand massaged my Yoni, but unlike my experience with Rachel, it wasn't very pleasant. The focus wasn't on bringing me to an orgasmic state, but to reach a situation in which my Yoni was relaxed. Somehow, during the treatment, every spot Sanand touched, every angle, every depth, even when it was done with the utmost gentleness, caused me pain. She would insert her finger and I would cry or shout or swear.

"Try a different sound, move, move the energy," she would encourage me. And sure enough, at one point a place that had been painful suddenly became pleasurable. It was as if we had converted the pain, released it, and discovered pleasure hiding beneath.

The change brought about by Sanand's treatments was immediate. All that emotional baggage I had been lugging around was suddenly left behind, and I experienced a similar release in other places as well. I felt more at ease with my body and was less embarrassed, as if until that moment a dybbuk had been screaming inside my head: "Why are you pretending to be happy and fulfilled? You have no sex life!" The communication in bed between Alon and me improved, my Yoni was more relaxed, and I felt freer and less stressed. Finally, I could communicate my likes and dislikes—what I wanted and what I didn't.

Despite this progress, a lot of work still lay ahead. My sexual encounters with Alon created less conflict, but I still wasn't truly enjoying them. A few months later I felt ready for further investigation. After healing some of the wounds, I was eager to experience pleasure and bring it into my life.

"I must go to a sexuality workshop, the one Shahar told us about. It's time for the next step in the process, and I'd be really happy if you came with me," I said to Alon.

"No way," he immediately responded.

For several months we discussed, disagreed, and outright fought over this issue. Knowing that it was important to me didn't stop Alon from objecting to it. He didn't like the idea of working on our sexuality together with other participants in a workshop. To him it was a distraction that was liable to lead us backwards. He was concerned that it would create a new list of demands, and now that we were finally going to bed without fighting, why introduce another obstacle?

After a few months of being at each other's throats, but following a not-bad sexual encounter one evening, Alon told me he was reconsidering the workshop. He had also objected to Sanand at first, before admitting that our sessions with her had helped our relationship. Moreover, Shahar was one of the workshop facilitators, which Alon hoped might make him feel more at ease.

We were just planning our honeymoon in America. As fate would have it, there was a workshop in one of the places on our itinerary. We agreed that since we would be there for a month, and it was a six-day workshop, Alon would decide day-by-day whether or not to join.

In the meantime, we prepared for the scenario of him joining. I paid his participation fee, half of which wouldn't be reimbursed if we cancelled. Apart from registering, we didn't know how to prepare for such a workshop. When we asked Shahar, he suggested that we define our boundaries, that is, decide what we agreed on. For example, would it be acceptable if one of us touched someone else in the exercises? The answer to that question was an immediate 'No' from both of us. Alon and I would touch no one in that workshop but each other.

In April of that year we set out on our honeymoon destination: Lake Atitlan in Guatemala. This lake is located inside an ancient volcanic crater and is considered the deepest lake in Central America. The population there is a mix of older tourists, young backpackers and the local villagers, who belong to various tribes— all descendants of the Maya. The easiest way to move around is via boats that leave throughout the day. Apart from restaurants and shops, the villages offer a selection of yoga and meditation workshops, and cocoa ceremonies.

I was returning to the lake I had visited on my post-army trip, where I underwent forty-days of silence and practiced lucid dreaming. It was at that lake that I first asked myself the big questions: What is my purpose in the world? How can I find a way to both make a living and make the world a better place? For me the sexuality workshop was a natural continuation of this quest.

Alon had not officially let me know whether he was going to participate, but two days before the workshop, he started talking about all the logistics in the plural: "we" would go to the workshop, "we" would sleep in a double room, "we" would eat vegetarian food for a week. Apparently, he had chosen to join me. Still, I went with my intuition and didn't ask outright; it was a sensitive topic, and he could still change his mind.

The workshop was held in a yurt-like construction with a roof and glass walls overlooking a lake. The group included forty people, was gender balanced, and most of the participants looked around the ages of 35-40. People came to the workshop from the U.S., Europe, Latin America and Asia. When we first arrived, we waited with the others to check in. There was palpable tension in the air. People extended reserved smiles and murmured hello, barely making eye contact. No one knew what awaited us.

The first day was focused on getting to know each other through emotional sharing and movement. In the first exercise we were divided into smaller groups and asked to take off certain articles of clothing as part of the introduction. People chose mostly to take off their shirts, as if preparing for a swim.

Alon and I had a beautiful double room and even though we were part of the group, the atmosphere was romantic and tension-free. We felt as if we were continuing our honeymoon with the addition of some group dynamic exercises. But on the second evening, we found ourselves in the deep end.

"Ultimately, each person is responsible for their own pleasure," said one of the facilitators. "So each person needs to know their body and what gives them pleasure."

"I recommend taking some time each day for pleasuring yourselves," said another facilitator. "It's like working out or meditation. Our next exercise will be dedicated to such an activity."

We were all lying on a mattress with our eyes closed, and covered by a blanket. The room was completely dark except for the flicker of candles. The three facilitators spoke in turn, combining guided imagination and meditation. Relaxing music was playing in the background.

"Begin by stroking your right leg. Think how wonderful it is that you have a healthy leg to lead you around in the world," said one of them. "Stroke it from the top to the bottom and feel what kind of touch your leg likes. Maybe it wants you to press on it hard, maybe softly. Try to discover what works and give your leg what it deserves."

In this pleasant manner we explored our various body parts for about forty minutes, until we reached our stomachs. Another facilitator took the microphone and carried on.

"Listen to the sound of your stomach. Stroke it clock-wise and learn how your fingers can give it pleasure. Think of the service our stomach does for us each day and see how we can return the favor by offering pleasurable touch."

Only after we had touched our body parts were we invited to move to our sexual organs. At this point the music changed and became more rhythmic.

"Everyone knows how they like to touch their sexual organ, but if you don't you'll have a chance to explore it this evening, and to try out new things," said the facilitator.

"There's time, no one's looking at you, it's just you and your sexual organ. Give it what it needs."

I knew no one could see me because the room was dark. Every participant built a sort of nest for herself assembled of blankets, cushions and a mattress that created a private space, and everyone's eyes were closed, concentrating on themselves, myself included. I didn't experience an orgasm but it felt good.

"Focus on your body and on what it's asking for," said the facilitator. "If you feel your mind escaping to fantasies in order to heighten the pleasure, bring your attention back to your body."

I tried to carefully follow the instructions. Twice during the half-hour exercise, I stopped listening to the facilitators, opened my eyes, and tried to see how Alon was doing. Even though I knew where his nest was, it was hard for me to make him out. When the exercise was over and the lights back on, I approached Alon, who was lying on his side. His expression was angry and his body motionless.

When our eyes met, I smiled at him. He looked away, got up from the mattress, left the hall and started walking up the path leading to our room. Uh oh, here it comes, I thought to myself.

OUR ROOM WAS AT THE TOP OF A STEEP HILL AND THE PATH LEADING THERE WAS DARK. "Alon!" I shouted, hurrying after him, but he didn't even slow down. "Alon, wait up!" Every time I called out to him he picked up his pace. I tried to catch up, but I was still dizzy from the session, and soon he disappeared from view. I kept going, trying to let my eyes adjust to the dark. The path was stony and I was afraid I'd fall. When I reached the room Alon was sitting curled up on the sofa, staring into space.

"What's wrong? How are you?" I asked but he didn't answer. "Talk to me, please," I begged. I offered him a glass of water; he shook his head. I sat down and hugged my legs. Alon got up and took to the sofa opposite me.

After about ten minutes, he found his tongue: "That was so awful. I don't know what to do, I don't know what to do, I want to get out of here, I want to get out of here..." he whispered to himself over and over again, holding his head in his hands and starting to cry, still avoiding my face.

"Alon, everything's OK. We're together. We'll do whatever you want. I want to understand what happened," I said, taking his hand.

At these words, he agreed to look me in the eye and took a sip of water. He stood up and started to pace the room. "It was disgusting and I had to pee the whole time, and couldn't get up."

That was the last thing I had expected to hear. "So why didn't you go to the bathroom?"

"Because I didn't think I was allowed to, I felt trapped in that miserable situation. Being told how to touch myself? With dozens of people in the same room? It's disgusting. What does it have to do with anything? It's like being in some satanic cult. And the facilitators, I don't trust them. This isn't for me, I've got to get out of here, I want us to be on a boat first thing tomorrow morning." He stopped pacing, stood still, looked me in the eye and repeated: "I have to get out of this place."

I was shattered. My dream was shattered. I had so wanted us to practice sexuality together, learn and move forward. I was equally scared that one of us would go in a different direction and we would end up losing each other. And here, it was happening — Alon wanted to leave and I wanted to stay.

But I had to remain in that workshop, with or without him. Had to find the source that had held me back sexually my whole life. I wanted a life that included pleasure, I couldn't go on living with this constriction.

Summoning the courage, I said: "I want to stay. Is that OK with you?"

He started walking in circles again, clutching his head every few seconds. After a few minutes he looked at me and said: "I didn't choose to be here. I followed you. It's not fair that I should be stuck here at this lake while you do the workshop."

"I didn't force you to come here," I said, my tone becoming more assertive. "You chose to come. You can do other things until I'm done. There's a meditation center here, there are a ton of Israelis, there are hostels, there's even a town that we haven't visited yet. You can find ways to amuse yourself."

After another few minutes of silence, I gathered the courage again and added: "You could also decide to stay here with me and do only the exercises you feel comfortable doing. You enjoyed the ones from yesterday, didn't you?"

I didn't try to meet his eyes again, and Alon didn't say a word, only sat silently with his face to the window. To him the agonizing experience he had gone through was my doing. I felt helpless. Whatever course of action I chose would hurt one of us.

AND THEN I REMEMBERED THE TECHNIQUES WE HAD BEEN TAUGHT FOR EMOTIONAL RELEASE. We all have emotions that build up throughout the day, and sometimes they boil over. That's how it was explained to us. Cautiously optimistic, I chose the technique created by Osho, which is called emotional release. In this exercise, one person conducts a dialogue on her own, speaking both parts.

I stood up from the sofa, placed two pillows on the bed, sat down on one of them and, without warning, just started talking to Alon; but instead of looking at him I looked at the pillow in front of me.

"I'm angry. I'm disappointed. I'm scared. We're finally here. Let's do this together. Why are you pulling back?" With every sentence my tone grew stronger, until I was pounding the mattress with my fists. "I feel so paralyzed, I don't know what to do. I've got so many feelings of guilt and disappointment and anger. It's too much. Why can't you trust the process?" I yelled, punching away.

WHEN I RAN OUT OF THINGS TO SAY, I, TURNED TO THE OTHER PILLOW TO EXPRESS ALON'S PERSPECTIVE. "Why do I have to be here? What is this crap? *This is our honeymoon?* Why did you bring me to this mental institution? What do you have in common with all these psychos? Don't you realize I've just been through a trauma?" While I was Alon I paced the room as he had done earlier, waving my hands and holding my head in my hands. "Do you even realize I'm in a bad state? How dare you try to convince me to stay and give it another try? What is this? What?!" I cried and stomped my legs on the floor.

I peeked up at Alon. To my surprise, he had a smile on his face. He was amused by the situation. I continued role-playing for a few more rounds, verbalizing our frustration with each other, the gaps, my strong desire to stay, his to flee, the misery Alon was experiencing, and the sense of possibility and wonder that the workshop was giving me. I screamed both of us, cried both of us and even laughed a little, until I was spent and collapsed on the bed. Alon came over and lay down next to me. He hugged me.

"What do you think?" I asked in a whisper. There are some subjects we always talk about in a whisper, even if we're alone in a room.

"I don't know what I think," Alon whispered back. "All I know is that I can't stay here."

We continued hugging. His arms enfolded me, and my head leaned on his shoulder just the way I liked. It wasn't clear what we would do, but hugging was a good start. For about half an hour I was at peace with the situation. But then my anger started up again. I remembered how much I wanted this. For me. For us.

"Maybe you could at least talk with Shahar?" I suggested.

"To say what?"

"Just share how you're feeling."

"Fine," Alon agreed. "It won't help and I don't want him to try and convince me to stay, but you can call him."

I walked down the dark path, this time with a flashlight, until I found Shahar's room. I knocked on the door. He opened it, surprised.

"I need your help," I said with tears in my eyes. "Alon wants to leave. Can you try talking to him?"

While Alon and I lay in the hammock outside, Shahar sat in a chair next to us, listening to Alon tell him about his experience.

He listened quietly, even when Alon said he didn't trust the facilitators, not even him, and that he didn't believe in this framework and had to get the hell out of there and move to somewhere safe.

After Alon said his say, it was Shahar's turn: "I hear you. This is your experience, this is your story, and I respect it," he began. "But as a friend, let me say that I think there is a wound here, something you're afraid of reopening. Maybe you're not even aware of it. Maybe you feel shame toward your own sexuality, or of another's. I can't fully articulate it, but my gut tells me that not only should you stay here and explore your sexuality, but that you're going to choose to go deeper into this realm and perhaps even facilitate other people in the future."

Speechless, Alon and I looked at Shahar, and within a few seconds the three of us burst into laughter.

Alon still wanted to leave, but we convinced him to wait until morning and talk to the two other facilitators. We lay down in bed and closed our eyes. As usual, I placed my head in the space between Alon's neck and shoulder and we hugged. We were exhausted and still without a solution, but sleep was calling.

Unlike the conversation with Shahar, who is also our friend, Alon was not interested in having a dialogue with the other facilitators. When he described what state the workshop had left him in, one of the facilitators explained that as autonomous entities, we have to take responsibility for our feelings and experiences. The other facilitator suggested that Alon engage in introspection, to identify what had triggered him; maybe there was something deep inside him that needed addressing?

At this perceived evasiveness, Alon burst out: "Don't you realize how irresponsible you're being, leading all these exercises without considering the effects it can have on people?!"

Each person is free to do only the exercises she or he chooses, they went on. Alon wouldn't accept that explanation, either. I cried throughout the conversation, seeing it was going nowhere and realizing that I would either have to give up on pursuing my sexual development, or on Alon. Both options terrified me.

The workshop group was separated into "pods" — smaller groups comprised of six participants and one facilitator. At the start and end of each day the pods met to share their thoughts and feelings.

After the talk with the facilitators, Alon and I sat down to have breakfast. We didn't talk. After a few minutes he broke the silence to tell me he would say goodbye to his morning pod and then take the first boat out.

"Come with me, or don't come with me, it makes no difference anymore," he said, staring down at his plate of food.

We parted ways, each joining our respective pods.

At my pod's gathering, I fell apart. I told everyone how scared I was of staying without Alon, but also that I didn't want to leave in the middle. But who would I do the exercises with? I didn't want to practice with other people. And what if the gap between us stretched to the point of a separation? But to leave early? That would mean bad sex forever.

When the circle of sharing was over, I looked for Alon and saw that he was in the middle of a conversation with another person in his pod. I hoped that meant he had also gone through something meaningful in the circle.

I went into the main hall. There was music playing. Everyone was dancing but I looked on like a wallflower from the side. I was still broken up after the talk and didn't know what words still awaited me.

Suddenly, Alon came into the room and headed to the dance floor. He moved with reserve, but it was a drastic improvement from yesterday's restraint. I joined him, no questions asked. Alon stayed for the day's opening session, which was mostly instructive. We held hands the whole time.

At lunch he told me that he had cried while sharing his frustration and fears. Unlike the facilitators, his pod members didn't suggest that the problem was him or go on the defense. They supported him, and as a result he decided to stay, albeit on his own terms. He told the head facilitator that some exercises he would participate in, and some he would sit out. Simple. The facilitator agreed.

And so we spent the remaining days in the workshop: What we could do as a couple we did together and the rest of the time we gave each other the space we needed.

ONE OF THE EXERCISES WE PRACTICED TOGETHER WAS A YONI MASSAGE. At first, every spot Alon touched yielded a burning sensation. When an unpleasant sensation arose, we were supposed to take a deep breath and press the finger deeper into our Yoni. Just like the sessions with Sanand, even though it was now with my husband, my Yoni resisted the process. When his finger entered my Yoni, the whole area stiffened, and wanted to close up shop. Buzz off! I'm dry and uncomfortable. At a spot called "three in the afternoon," Alon paused.

"Breathe, make a sound, a movement, something," he "encouraged" me. This, in a room with twenty couples. I tried to pant, which was more than a little awkward. Alon pushed his finger in deeper while looking into my eyes. I love his eyes but at that particular moment I wanted to chop his finger off. At one point, the women near me started making noises. I tried a moan. Encouraged, Alon pushed his finger further in. Then farther. I froze.

"Try to relax," he said. Only a few days ago he had wanted to hop on the first boat back, and now suddenly he was sounding like a new-age therapist. I was furious.

"Stop," I snapped.

Alon decided to move to another spot. Here everything was hard, a minefield, fire, as if a knife had come into contact with my

Yoni, even though Alon's finger was in the most delicate position possible. I hardened my Yoni, as though placing blockades around his finger: "No Entrance." The song playing in the background was becoming more rhythmic and I, more angry.

"Try to relax," said the spiritual guru in front of me who, only a few moments ago, had been my husband, the level-headed accountant.

"Don't tell me what to do! Shut up!!!" I screamed, surprising the both of us.

Alon glanced at the facilitator, who gave him an empathetic nod, and then looked back at me. His compassionate expression moved me so much, I burst into tears.

While I cried, tears also filled Alon's eyes. He put his finger further inside me, and it burned less. I cried, even shouted, as he pushed his finger farther in. The song changed. The Yoni started to soften. This man in front of me — as if he had been doing this for years, said: "There, we're opening up." He was referring to the fluids released.

It started with a giggle, but then my whole body joined in and it became a full-blown laugh. I couldn't stop. Alon smiled awkwardly, glanced at the facilitator again for a signal, then moved to "nine in the morning." The burning sensation was almost gone, and as the song changed again, I heard a few women in the room start to laugh as well. It was contagious. Suddenly my body experienced a pleasant ticklish sensation. Alon moved to "12 noon" and another burst of pleasure came, followed by another. As he moved around this entire clock, which is my Yoni, everything became wet. It wasn't an orgasm per se, but it was definitely pleasure. I couldn't tell which were his fingers and which was my Yoni — it all became one.

"I love you, my love," I exhaled. The exercise was over; Alon made to remove his finger. "No, no, no, please don't go," I begged him.

PEOPLE IMAGINE THAT YOU LEARN POSITIONS FROM THE KAMA SUTRA or scenes out of porn movies at a sexuality workshop, but this workshop was much more than that. It included learning to recognize when something feels good and when it borders on invasive; sacred sexuality ceremonies; techniques to give the Yoni and the Lingam a healing touch. In a large dark room, separated into couples, in an atmosphere that was clean, pure and respectful, with tribal music and gentle guidance, we all worked on healing our deep inner wounds. While lying on the mattress, or sitting and offering Alon my touch, I heard people shouting, crying, rolling with laughter—dozens of voices all at once.

The workshop also included collective healing of women's personal traumas.

A participant who had been sexually abused as a child said she wanted to use the safe space created by the group to regain her trust in men. As she stood in the middle of the circle and described the assault, the facilitator seated five men around her in an inner circle to listen. Before she finished speaking we were already crying, and then she signaled to one of the men to come closer and ended the story hugging him and weeping in his arms.

The intimate situations generated in the group felt natural to me. They evoked a primal memory, as if I had been in temples like this in a previous life. It reminded me of that feminine quality that had accompanied me in the women's circles; its energy coursed through me, and my heart expanded to the greater part I play as a woman in this world. It became second nature to go through these processes in a community - immersed in working with the body, healing sexuality and practicing radical sincerity for an entire week with forty strangers. Our sexual gates were beginning to open.

IT WAS WORTH FIGHTING FOR THIS WORKSHOP. Despite its group nature, the workshop was first and foremost a personal process each woman underwent with herself. On top of the deep emotional exercises and the connection to our bodies, we also looked honestly at what we really wanted, and from this place reached decisions in aspects of our lives that at first may not seem directly linked to sexuality.

One of the things they taught us was the concept: "If it's not a hell yes, then it's a no."

To reach any decision, a person needs to arrive at a "yes" on three levels: the mind, the heart and the body. What I think I'm supposed to do, what I feel a need to do and what my body is telling me to do. From the moment I learned that, and to listen to my body, many of the cognitive loops that would emerge while trying to make a decision disappeared. I understood that there is always one right and true option.

Following the workshop, I resisted expending even the slightest amount of energy in something that was not "true." To my surprise, the place I felt my sexual awakening most acutely was in my career.

CHAPTER 3
WHY ARE YOU CLOSING?

"Without community, there is no liberation."
Audre Lorde

I GOT STRAIGHT BACK TO OUR STARTUP AFTER THE WORKSHOP. Even though we were well underway to reaping the fruits of three years of toil, the workshop reinforced my nagging conviction that my place wasn't there. If I was honest with myself, the only thing that had really moved me during the past few years was the program we had created for women. Prior to the workshop, this thought would only arise in the rare moments that I had time to think, but after it, something in me awakened, demanding attention. Before the workshop I could sit through hours of meetings or conversations that didn't interest me. After I returned, even five minutes was five minutes too many.

Although I knew leaving was inevitable, it wasn't simple. I had commitments to investors, clients, students, my partner and my team — all people I loved and appreciated.

Two weeks after our return, my partner Avi called to tell me we needed to travel to Ukraine to meet with potential investors. While he spoke about the trip, I leafed through my calendar and saw all the events I was going to miss in Israel: a friend's birthday, a family dinner and a lecture I was supposed to give at a Google campus gathering. Each one of these activities was more important to me than this trip.

As always, a strong voice inside me said: why don't you just say yes and be done with it? What do you care? Just this one last time and then you'll have the talk about the future. Do what's right for the business. It's important. Be mature, considerate. Why should he go alone? Be the partner he needs. My body, which I had only recently learned to listen to, was crying out from inside: 'Noooo.... Please don't take me there. I don't want to go!'

I started mumbling: "Of course I'll come if it's necessary, no question, but maybe it would be better if I attended the meetings on video? After all, someone has to stay here with the sales team... it's important that I be here... And we haven't prepared for this... and there's also the matter of the expense..." I shifted uncomfortably in my seat.

Alon, who was with me in the car, asked me to put the phone on mute.

"Hang on a sec," I said to Avi. And Alon said to me: "Cut the bullshit — just tell him the truth."

I mustered my courage, unmuted the phone and told Avi: "I won't be coming with you."

"What? Why?" he asked in surprise.

"Because I don't want to and because my body is signaling to me that this is the right decision."

Silence on the other end. We wished each other a good day and hung up.

Breathing a sigh of relief, I looked at Alon. We both smiled. Since returning home, we had grown closer, our relationship stronger. We still had a distance to go, but that pre-taste of sexual fulfilment in the workshop exercises had put us on the right track. In the meantime, we had a tacit understanding to watch over each other, lest we stray from our paths. I felt victorious. I didn't think about the implications or what would happen tomorrow. It was Independence Day in Israel, and I was celebrating my own.

WHEN I GOT TO THE OFFICE THE NEXT DAY, AVI SAT ME DOWN. He informed me that it might be time for us to stop working together. I had already said in the past that I was thinking of leaving, that it didn't seem like a startup I should lead, that I wanted to pursue other things. Over the past few months I'd initiated a similar conversation once a week. As long as I went on doing my job, from his end everything was fine. He allowed me my ambivalence, attributing it to my millennial personality, but if this wavering meant not fulfilling my responsibilities as a business partner, especially during the critical time of fundraising, that was crossing the line.

He said: "Make a decision one way or another. Enough with all the talk about leaving. Are you staying or not?"

I replied: "I guess it really is time for me to leave."

It was deceptively easy to utter those words; For over a year I had known I needed to leave the startup. But no matter how certain I was about this decision, it was still a goodbye, and it hurt — either they were giving up on me in a business I had helped build, or I was forgoing future accomplishments.

Although we parted respectfully, and I knew he would continue taking the business forward, and even though my whole body told me it was the right decision, I still experienced grief. My identity had been stripped away, leaving me with no direction. And I had been ejected from the exclusive startup club.

But there was one element of our startup that would stay with me — the women's desert workshop. Immediately after I returned, we convened another one, comprised of one hundred women from fourteen countries. I was fortunate to witness the changes that the participants underwent: some made important career decisions; some found the courage to relocate; some finally dared to raise funds for their project; and some — myself included — set out to develop a deeper relationship with their body and partners. Strong friendships formed, some of which even evolved into business partnerships.

This project showed me what it meant to be a woman, and how to harness the power that can be found in the feminine. The growth (both sexual and emotional) that it engendered made it clear that even though I was leaving the startup, Sarah and I would continue spearheading this project.

In the negotiations with the investors and my partner concerning my departure, each side made concessions and we managed to reach an arrangement that was acceptable to everyone. Sarah and I would continue creating entrepreneurial programs for women, but to avoid confusion we would devise a program that was different from the one associated with the startup, both in terms of branding and content. The result? The launching of a women's workshops program that we called "Double You," which refers both to the "w" in "women," and to the concept of doubling yourself.

I strove for financial independence the year of my sexual awakening. In the summer of 2016, a few months after the workshop, I started my own company. The process I had been through had released the creativity and courage needed to realize a vision that until now had remained dormant. Even though I had already founded two small businesses, I had always been the one who "joined the team," who adapted to an existing structure and advanced it from there. This time I spread my wings. It was the first time I had said, with trembling knees, "This is the way — follow me."

In our previous workshops Sarah and I had imposed limitations to the incorporation of mind-body content, compelled to remain relevant to the expectations of the (often cynical) startup industry. Now that we were reinventing the wheel, I knew that we could take things much further.

Sharing my enthusiasm about the sexuality workshop, I explained to Sarah how significant it was to my career, my confidence, my ability to say "no" more easily, how I no longer froze when men made questionable comments.

"I believe there are tools every woman should acquire, and they have a direct impact on our ability to lead and progress," I told her.

Nodding, Sarah said supportively: "I know exactly what you're talking about. Let's call it 'The Red Tent'."

We had more questions than answers when it came to thinking about the right way to integrate elements from sexuality workshops into a workshop for female entrepreneurs; but we had experience under our belts, and it would undoubtedly be less complicated than the workshop Alon and I had made it through, not to mention there would be only women in the room, so what could go wrong? We were both used to figuring things out on the move, in line with the startup methodology of letting the customer encounter the product before it was ready, in order to receive feedback and improve it. Later we learned that this methodology proved less effective when it came to the human psyche.

THE FIRST "RED TENT" WORKSHOP TOOK PLACE IN THE NORTH OF ISRAEL. It was attended by eighty women whose day-to-day lives were very intense, often involving pursuing ambitious careers while raising children. Nevertheless, they decided to take three days off in order to develop their entrepreneurial ideas.

The rules of the workshop dictated complete detachment from the outside world. The participants were required to give us their phones and wear the clothes we gave them. They also couldn't share where they were from or what their professions were until the workshop was over. These rules were intended to avoid comparison-making and to encourage focusing on the reason they had signed up: to develop their entrepreneurial visions.

We didn't publish the schedule beforehand. "Let yourself be surprised," we encouraged. "Come and take a leap into the unknown, on an authentic entrepreneurial journey." We promised the participants a supportive space that would make their time worthwhile: three days for thinking about their projects and building up the confidence required to realize them.

We set up an actual red tent at the workshop. With red fabric Sarah had found at the Carmel Market, scented candles, stones in the center of the room, and dozens of cushions, the space invited women to discover and explore their own bodies. I invited Sanand, our sexual therapist, to facilitate the activities focusing on sexuality and desire.

At the end of a lesson-packed day, which required the participants to arrive at crucial decisions about the idea they were developing, the women gathered in the cozy, mattress-lined room where Sanand led workshops focused on sacred poetry, reconnecting us to the womb and channeling the female and male energies that existed in each one of us.

On the first evening, the participants were asked to arrange themselves in a human mandala formed by concentric circles of women. Each woman in the inner circle had to lean against the back of a woman in the outer circle. We were guided to absorb each other's breathing while repeating the sounds that Sanand had taught us, thereby creating a circle of sacred poetry. While an awkward first for most of the women, the exercise seemed to go smoothly, and the feedback was positive.

When it came to the other Red Tent lessons, opinions were divided. In a session intended to help the participants distinguish between their male and female energies, they were asked to walk across the room in a straight line and then in a circle. In another session focused on connecting with the womb, there was a guided imagination exercise that led them along the paths of their womb.

Some of the participants welcomed this exposure to new concepts, and the prospect of becoming better acquainted with their bodies, even if they didn't fully understand how it related to their project. Others claimed these activities had nothing to do with being an entrepreneur and that they hadn't invested their valuable time and money for this sort of spectacle.

We were prepared for such criticism. Whenever you test unchartered water, there will inevitably be skeptics. At his famous Harvard University lecture, Steve Jobs spoke about the need of entrepreneurs to face the critics and faultfinders with determination. But this was not our main challenge — that came from women we hadn't even taken into account when we designed the Red Tent. For some, the focus on sexuality brought up difficult experiences from the past. Looking back, I realize that it was precisely for these women that we had set out on this journey in the first place.

IN THE COURSE OF THE WORKSHOP, WOMEN STARTED SHARING PERSONAL STORIES ABOUT SEXUAL HARASSMENT in the hi-tech industry. This was before the #MeToo era, when the topic of sexual harassment in hi-tech and start-ups still existed in a grey zone and was not a topic for discussion. But the moment we began addressing the subject of the body, the stories started pouring out.

After the workshop we started a closed Facebook group and created a community to share content, professional tools and networking events. The subject of dealing with sexuality and especially sexual harassment arose time and again. It was as if a Pandora's box had opened up.

At the time, we were filming a video blog for our public Facebook page in order to expand the circle of women exposed to our content. We interviewed women in the community who shared how they had started their enterprise, offered tips for fundraising, obtaining resources and more. To save on equipment and filming costs, we scheduled long shooting days at Dana's apartment, who was a member of the community, and the other members would file in one after the other. It was a bright apartment with a grey floor, white sofas, a light brown rug and a kitchen island you could sit around and chat. A make-up artist for the shoot and those who were waiting or had just finished did just that—sat around and chatted.

During one lunchbreak, Sivan, an entrepreneur who had attended our last workshop, told us she was going to close her startup. I was surprised, because she had serious and well-known industry investors, had won awards, boasted customers, and her product was being reviewed in leading international newspapers.

"What happened?" I asked.

"Fundraising is too difficult," she replied. "So I decided to give it up."

"Is that really why?" I wondered. "Let's get you in touch with other investors, I'm sure you'll find some takers."

"I don't have the energy," insisted Sivan. "I've had enough meetings with investors."

Tal, who was working for McKinsey and whose work routine included periods of intensive work with breaks in between, said, "Maybe you need some time off? Go to the desert and you'll come back recharged."

"No," Sivan said determinedly. "It won't help."

"Have you considered crowdfunding?" suggested Dana.

"It's just that I'm doing all the fundraising alone," she said, almost in a whisper. "Most of the investors are men and it creates unpleasant situations…" she trailed off. "I'd just rather stop."

"What happened, Sivan?" I asked, encouraging her to sit down. But she remained standing.

Silence in the living room.

"A very senior investor... harassed me... in the middle of a business meeting," she lowered her gaze.

"I think I know who it is," said Dana and mentioned his name.

"How did you know?" Sivan asked, astounded.

"I've also heard similar things," I said, and Tal confirmed with her look that she had too.

"So let's do something about it," declared Tal.

"It's too complicated. I'd just rather stop meeting with investors, and I don't want to talk about him with other people," said Sivan.

"We don't have to talk about him personally. The fact that a phenomenon like this exists is wrong. He's definitely not the only one. Did you hear how many stories came up in the last retreat? Let's talk about it in the interview," I suggested. "There are other women who have had the same experience and you could help them. Just don't mention names," I said.

Originally, we had planned to speak with Sivan about launching a product abroad. At the beginning of the interview we discussed her business, but the focus quickly shifted to her experience of sexual harassment. Sivan described how her first meeting with the investor had been professional and to the point. At the second meeting they already realized the investment was not relevant to his investment fund, but they continued discussing other business collaboration ideas. Then, one evening, they met in a busy café. She thought it would be fine. She had a coffee, he a beer, and suddenly, mid-sentence, he put his hand on her leg. She froze and gently moved away. He tried again. She said: "I have to go." He followed her out and called after her; when she turned around he tried to kiss her. She pushed him away and ran off.

Sivan blamed herself for what happened, and berated herself with questions: Did I put too much passion into my pitch? Maybe coming off as so enthusiastic about my project conveys the wrong message? At that point, she called it quits with the investors—and with her startup.

Following this video and other actions taken by other brave women, stories about senior personnel in the industry led to investigative journalistic news items that exposed the man's identity. They invited us to come forward. At first, we considered collaborating with the journalists, but talking with the media researchers put the living fear into us: they warned us that our phones might be tapped, pressured us to give them names, and demanded being put in touch with other women. Most of the women in the community wanted their stories kept out of the media, and the last thing we wanted was to jeopardize the safe space we were trying to create.

The responsibility we had taken upon ourselves began to weigh on us: from the moment our focus shifted to feminine sexuality at the workshops, painful stories started pouring in from women in the community. We felt we didn't have the tools to deal with the complexity of the situation and considered switching gears.

IN THE MEANTIME, IN MY PERSONAL LIFE, OUR SEXUALITY HAD ALREADY SWITCHED GEARS. We still hadn't learned how to make me come, but we had hope. We received tools which helped us navigate the places where we used to get stuck. For example, when I was in that state of disorientation that inhibited my pleasure, instead of freezing I would pause, look into Alon's eyes and say, "Stop a second, be with me. I want us to be in the same rhythm." Alon would look straight into my eyes and slow his movements. This would bring me back to the room. If at that moment I didn't want to continue, even though Alon hadn't come yet, instead of stopping in protest I'd say I preferred to stop while lovingly holding his Lingam. If this upset him, I'd invite him to talk about it and we would work through it together. Sometimes

Alon didn't feel like talking, and he would kiss me sensually to get me to keep going. Sometimes it worked. Other times he was the one who had to release his dependency on coming and he would channel the energy to other parts of his body. We learned to meet in bed with less expectation and to let go of the tasks that "had" to be completed for the sex to be considered a success. This created diverse sexual encounters in which all sorts of things could happen, and where sometimes stroking each other was the main event.

At this point, everyone close to us knew that our honeymoon had taken us to a sexuality workshop and that it had changed our lives. This included our parents. Like any mother and father, they wanted their children to be happy. When we raved about the workshop, they smiled and refrained from asking questions. When friends heard where we had been, they smiled awkwardly, cracked some dirty joke and changed the subject.

We started attending advanced workshops.

At the first session, we decided there were certain things we wanted to practice with other people within clear boundaries: no French kissing, no touching of sexual organs and of course no penetration. It started with a small exercise, in which one hand touched another's, or looking into another's eyes. Closer contact followed: touching someone while dancing at a changing rhythm set by the facilitator, or running our hand along someone's body with the aim of learning to be attentive to other people's boundaries—and to pay attention: is the person in front of us actually interested in this? Am I? If a sign suggested otherwise, we were required to acknowledge it and move on. All the experiences in the workshop were accompanied by transparent and open communication, each of us free to change our minds at any given moment.

This process heightened the sexual tension between us—but in a good way. We discovered that some things turned us on only with new people with whom we had no existing habits or preconceptions about. To our delight, what excited us with others remained exciting when we were alone. Dancing sensually with another man made me feel light and desirable. Later, when I danced with Alon, I charged at him like a predator, kissing all the body parts available to me. It was a fascinating transformation.

The workshop was a safe space for such experiences, because its main and professed objective was the participant's personal evolution. There were very clear rules and boundaries that prevented us from falling back on "being horny" or pursuing the conquest of others. It protected us.

These experiences allowed both of us to learn loads about our sexuality. Alon, for example, learned that for years he had been ashamed of his sexual urges. He thought their frequency made him a bad person. The workshop let him connect with his urges in a therapeutic way. I learned more about the reason I had come there — to better relate to my pleasure. It turned out the challenge of experiencing pleasure in a sexual encounter was connected to something much deeper than I had thought.

One day, during a Yoni ceremony, the facilitator demonstrated an exercise on another female facilitator. I noticed that if I was sitting at an angle that gave me a view of the latter's Yoni, I was disgusted. During the entire workshop, I was unable to look at it. It was much easier for me to look at the Lingam, which I found more aesthetic. The female sexual organ is a complicated structure with individual variations for each woman, and a range of colors and textures. I wasn't used to peering at it, not at my own and certainly not that of others. I assumed there was a direct link between this alienation and my detachment from my Yoni. I shared this insight with Alon and we decided that getting closer to my Yoni would become our mission. How could I want fulfillment as a woman without accepting the fact that I had a Yoni, that I had a vagina?

WE HAD A SIMILAR INSIGHT IN DOUBLE YOU. No matter how hard we tried to focus less on sexuality in the women's entrepreneurial workshops, it emerged again and again from all directions. The stories we heard from the community members, and the requests from both old and new participants for more discussion, kept multiplying. We were out of our depth in dealing with this explosive topic, but realized this was our calling.

Female sexuality suffers so much social repression, and when it's finally given room to express itself, the joy is often accompanied by pain. We realized the need to stay on this complex course, partly even because of the complexities involved. "One day the world will be ready to listen," we said to ourselves, "and then we'll be able to talk openly."

We continued offering the workshops with the Red Tent gatherings, and the more we progressed the deeper the engagement became. For example, at one of the workshops Rachel, an experienced sexuality facilitator, was guiding the group through a removal ceremony. Part of the ceremony involves symbolic gestures you make as a commitment to profound change. In this symbolic ceremony, each participant is asked to mention a particular behavior she would like to dispose of, and then to remove an article of clothing. For example: "I remove the need to be loved" or "I remove the need to apologize all the time."

In the first removal ceremony the women sat along a wall decorated with red fabric. Opposite them, a candlelit table was adorned with crystals and flowers. Rachel, with Danielle at her side — one of the other facilitators — stood by it. While taking their clothes off, the women poured their hearts out. Someone shared that she had had an abortion when she was twenty. "I wanted to keep the baby," she said, "but I was afraid of losing my partner, so I agreed. I want to remove the fear of being walked out on, which makes me agree to things I regret," she said and took off her shirt.

Another woman shared how fed up she was with having to take care of all the people in her life — her bosses, parents, partner and children, at the expense of herself. "I remove the need to be Mother Theresa or Superwoman!" she shouted and took off her shirt. "I remove the need to be perfect!" She unfastened her bra as tears rolled down her eyes. Clutching her breasts, she declared, "I love my breasts. I remove the will to hide them. They're beautiful." We all cried with her.

Women confided their medical problems, missed career opportunities, sexual harassment experiences and discrimination. They sang songs they had never sung out loud, shared projects they hadn't received credit for, successes they had kept from LinkedIn or even left off their CV. This ceremony was conducted in full or partial nudity, in front of the group. Physical and emotional nakedness. A deep baring of the soul. For most in the group, it proved to be a healing, moving and empowering experience.

Some of the women left the room in the middle of the ceremony. I told myself it was fine, that we're grown women, each one takes what she can and assumes responsibility for herself.

At the end of the evening, Maor, one of the participants, walked up to me and said: "I'd like to go home. I feel as if I've been violated." I was shocked. I, who had been sexually harassed for years, who was set on combating and confronting this issue, was now being accused of contributing to it.

"What?" is all I managed to utter.

"You didn't explain in advance that the workshop was going to touch on topics like these. I had no idea I was going to be exposed to the things the women here shared, least of all their nudity. I want to go home and think about what happened here this evening, and what to do next."

Everyone had already left the tent. It was just the two of us sitting on the floor, she with her legs crossed and me hugging my knees in discomfort. Angrily, Maor told me that as far as she was concerned what happened here tonight had crossed the line, and was the height of irresponsibility, We should have explained ahead of time that there would be nudity in the workshops, not say it was a "surprise" and simply let things happen.

Her reaction immediately reminded me of how Alon felt at the self-gratification ceremony in the first workshop we attended, but this time I was the workshop facilitator and the responsibility was mine. I was filled with shame.

Assuming full responsibility, I told her about the process we had gone through with the Red Tent. I explained the reasons for initiating the project in the first place. I told her how, after the first workshop, when we just touched on the subject, endless stories made their way to us and how, before each session, we reviewed the feedback and adjusted the content accordingly.

I told her I understood the importance of communicating that there would be nudity in the workshop, and that we thought implying it would take place was enough. I stressed that we felt we were on a mission — that female sexuality was repressed in the world, which blocked our access to a huge source of potential power, that society gives it expression only in the darkness, and we want to give it light.

"But you're not giving it light," she countered and added, "You want to take it out of the darkness, but you also did it in the darkness, without advance notice, by calling it a 'surprise,' and without explaining the context. You're doing the exact same thing out of shame. Hiding in the shadows."

I was quiet, letting what she had said sink in. A few moments later I said, "If we spelled things out in advance, it might put off some women who could stand to gain from it."

"Give the women you work with more credit, Narkis," she scoffed. "We're not little girls. In fact, you should do a little growing up if you're going to handle such sensitive topics."

I hung my head. Maor was 45, more than a decade older than me. I felt as if I had taken a scolding by an older sister.

"You know what, I think you're right. I see that now. This was not our intention. I'm really sorry."

She turned pensive, and then said, "I appreciate your honesty and the way you're taking responsibility. I'll think it over tonight."

The next morning, Maor said she had decided to stay but only on the condition that I told her exactly what was going to happen in the Red Tent that evening. I agreed.

When the workshop was over we thanked each other. We had both learned an important lesson, and she had become someone I continued to confer with about how to implement our content. We still had a long way to go before we could raise the flag and openly declare that we were exploring the interrelation between leadership and feminine sexuality.

By the end of that workshop, many unanswered questions remained: How was it that we had brought in experienced facilitators who knew how to hold space yet still made so many mistakes? Why did this topic evoke so much resistance in some women? Why did women who led a business, oversaw employees and made commitments to investors fear confronting their own sexuality?

We would have to find good answers to these questions, and communicate them to the participants in the following workshops, but where to start looking? There was still so much work to be done.

IN 2018 WE LAUNCHED A NEW WEBSITE. We didn't explicitly indicate that our focus was on sexuality, but the site was designed in a red color scheme and included photos and texts from the Red Tent. We wrote about working with the body and used words like "desire" and "getting in touch with your wild side."

In the preparatory calls we had with the enrollees, we explained that we were working with sexual energy, and that the workshop included methods for exploring sexuality and desire. We emphasized that it was only natural for each woman to relate differently to different parts, and that it was up to her to decide what to embrace and what not.

Soon after, a rumor began to circulate that our workshop was known as "the workshop where everyone got naked." I didn't think much of it. People liked to talk, and play "Telephone"; plus, we told ourselves that making a change in the world came with criticism and suffering generalizations. That said, we believed that the updated content on the website and the phone calls were sufficiently transparent. But a few days before the next workshop, one of the women who had signed up sent us the following email:

"Dear Double You Team,

I'm very excited about the upcoming workshop and I would like to clarify a couple of things beforehand. Some friends recently said something that troubled me. They claimed the workshop includes a mandatory session in which women are required to dance naked.

My first response to this information was disbelief. Later I thought that I would do only what I was comfortable with, but I'm still uneasy and would like to know in advance if this information is correct.

I'd appreciate a response so that I can feel comfortable about coming to the workshop.

Thanks,

Dana"

Back to the drawing board. We realized it wasn't enough to explain to participants on the phone what was on the agenda. If we didn't take responsibility for the way we told our story, someone else would tell it for us, and get it wrong. It was time for us to get it right.

One of the reasons I had delayed "getting the message right" about female sexuality was because I was scared. Until then I had been a social entrepreneur, and a nice ornament addition to any convention: I had lectured at the Foreign Office, the World Economic Forum in Davos, before the European Union Education Ministers and a small group of people that included the Prime Minister. I liked that status, feeling that I was Someone. I was afraid that the moment we declared what we actually did in Double You, I would be cast out of these forums and become No one.

Additionally, after leaving the startup, alongside heading Double You, I made a living from consultancy projects with CEOs and teams in startups on the subject of female leadership and organizational culture. I was invited because of my experience in establishing communities and creating content for women in Double You, but as far as those companies were concerned, what we provided at our workshops was leadership and entrepreneurial content; "sexuality" was not on the agenda. Those were the jobs I was worried about losing most of all, because beyond the fact that they paid the bills, they also met the most significant need I had back then — to be considered successful by men.

CHAPTER 4
I ALSO WANTED TO OPEN UP LIKE A FLOWER

"I realized that the hair is there for a reason — it's the leaf around the flower, the lawn around the house. You have to love the hair in order to love the vagina. You can't pick the parts you want."

Eve Ensler

MY DREAM WAS TO TEACH MALE CEOS TO GROW A WOMB IN BUSINESS INSTEAD OF A PAIR OF BALLS. Instead of aggressiveness and belligerence, I wanted to show that what was needed today were sensitive managers and entrepreneurs who connected to their inner selves. I started offering startup team workshops and progressive consultations on the subject of soft skills. Soon I had clients in Israel, Europe and America, both in the business and social worlds, and a hope that the CEOs would learn to trust me enough to let me add the contents I wanted to these workshops.

Influencing the way men think was greatly gratifying: unlike my previous company, the CEOs in these workshops were happy to hear me speak about "fluff" messages, empowerment and a sense of purpose. That was exactly why they had brought me there. I'd fly out once every six weeks to lecture or conduct workshops. The many hours I spent buckled in to my seat were ideal for dreaming about my business taking off, just like the airplane.

On the flights, I'd envision myself together with a group of female partners who would come on board as the activity expanded, travelling the world in pink suits, spreading our feminine doctrine wherever we went. We were in fact on a mission to spread femaleness across the globe. It started by partnering with startups, but we would be working with governments soon enough, restoring balance.

Daydreaming was one of my favorite activities. Before we had even crossed the Atlantic, our company already had branches across the world and millions in profit. My vision was so complete in my mind that I felt butterflies in my stomach, as if it was really happening.

In addition to traveling for work, I made a point to attend sexuality workshops in the area, taking advantage of the paid airfare. I jumped at any opportunity to lecture at a conference, any opportunity to receive clients abroad — my appetite was insatiable. This was my time, before having children, to build an empire and take the world by storm.

ONE DAY, MY GOOD FRIEND SAGIE CALLED and told me that he had a special arrangement with an airline company that could finance as many trips as my heart desired.

"If you pay an agent in the U.S. $7,000, he can put you in touch with an employee at one of the big airlines. They'll register you as their partner or best friend, and you can fly when and wherever you want, first class, for a whole year, depending on availability."

"What? That's crazy. But $7,000 is a lot of money."

"Did you hear what I just told you?" he said in disbelief. "You can fly wherever you want. You could make a spontaneous last-minute decision. I've been doing it for two months. It's like ordering a cab. It's changed my life. The potential income you could gain from a business encounter on a single flight far exceeds $7,000. Think big!"

Sagie was a young, successful entrepreneur, and after speaking with him I always felt as if I could grow wings and fly. I imagined myself in first class, making deals with CEOs of organizations who I could introduce to the world-embracing female organization that I was founding.

Alon didn't go for the idea.

"It sounds iffy," he said. "And why would you fly more than you already do? It's too much as is."

We talked it over. Finally, when I told him that I promised to pay back the money in installments from my business account, because they would be business trips anyhow, he gave in: "Do whatever you want," he shrugged.

Sagie put me in touch with an American agent named Eric who made the connection with the airline employee. I received written confirmation that he would pay back half the sum at any stage if I wasn't happy, and we struck the deal. I felt guilty for doing something that Alon didn't believe in, but I knew that he often objected because he was afraid, only to later agree that it was worth it. I decided to follow my instincts and excitement. If there's anything I took from those startup CEOs, it was the willingness to take a risk.

I KNOW VERY FEW PEOPLE UP FOR TAKING ON the risk involved in creating a startup, a business whose investors expect a return of seven or ten times their investment. The few entrepreneurs who are cut out for it tend to be people who thrive from these irrational conditions. They raise millions of dollars, tell a story that justifies it and won't stop until they reach the finish line, which means becoming a powerhouse company that can boast a billion-dollar net worth, minimum.

I wasn't like that, but in my consultancy career I had worked closely with CEOs who were, and admired them. I wanted to channel the courage, charisma and ability to think big from them. I wanted their attention, their approval, and for them to need me professionally.

This plane ticket, I thought to myself, would be my ticket to productivity. I could attend more conventions where CEOs of various organizations would be milling about, be spontaneous about making appointments, and meet more women who would join the team I was building. On top of all of that, I could also attend more workshops and expand my repertoire of adventure activities.

The ticket I purchased was called *Companion* and with it every destination in the world was at my disposal. From the moment I bought it my pattern of thinking changed and my ideas suddenly multiplied. While at first, I merely toyed with the notion, I started seeing each day as an opportunity to travel abroad.

Around the same time, David, one of my friends in the sexual studies community in Israel, scheduled a meeting with me. I was sure it would be about work. He had a business of his own and I assumed he wanted to ask me to give a workshop to the women in his organization.

We met at the Sarona Market in Tel Aviv. Over sushi, we talked about life. He told me he was considering doing one of the advanced sexuality workshops and was interested in hearing what went on there.

In the last session of the workshop he was asking about, they recommended not telling outsiders the details about it, lest they be misinterpreted and deter people from enrolling. Unlike our process in Double You, where the emphasis was on leadership and professional development, people who signed up for sexuality workshops knew about the deep sexual process that it entailed. No syllabus is provided in advance. Ahead of the workshop, members are asked to take responsibility for their experience, and while protecting their own boundaries, to relinquish control where possible.

"You're better off finding out for yourself," I said. "It'll help you experience the workshop the right way."

David pressed on. While he asked his questions I had flashbacks from that workshop. I saw frames from it, like something out of a movie, where Alon and I were in the role of animals; I remembered receiving a leaf from a tree that indicated who and what gender my partner would be for an exercise; I recalled a group of forty people dancing in ecstasy, even though they hadn't had anything to drink or smoke, intoxicated by life itself.

"It's very powerful," I said, returning to my body and the conversation.

"Anything else?" he implored.

"I'd really rather not go into detail," I said.

A silence settled between us. I realized that this was the reason for the meeting, and David wasn't going to get anything out of it.

"Well, I'll decide whether to sign up after I get back from Egypt," he finally said.

"Egypt? What are you doing in Egypt? I asked.

"In three weeks there's a Nile cruise with Seth, Jasmin and Jim."

"No way... Whoa... I know all those names—they're some of the leading facilitators in the world!" I couldn't contain my excitement. But aren't you afraid to go to Egypt?"

"I do my best to not let fear manage my life," David replied calmly.

Boom! What a sentence. It almost made me want to sign up for the cruise.

"Maybe Alon and I are meant to go on this trip?" I mused aloud.

David went on telling me about work, but I was no longer listening. A few minutes later I asked: "Are there even any flights from Israel to Egypt?"

"Every day," David laughed. "It's part of the peace treaty — even if there's just one person on the flight, it leaves from Ben Gurion Airport to Cairo."

I TOLD ALON ABOUT A NILE CRUISE on which we could practice sexuality with some of the best teachers in the world, and become more attuned with my Yoni.

"This could be the recipe for orgasm that we've been looking for! Plus, since it's a cruise, the schedule is probably less structured. It's not like we'll spend the whole day in sessions."

Alon smiled. He had enjoyed the workshops, but, leaving his comfort zone at such short notice would surely trigger his usual resistance.

"OK, let's do it," he said.

"What? Seriously?"

"Yes."

"You won't later say that I dragged you along against your will?"

"First look into it," Alon said, and smiled again.

I looked into it. Luckily, there were still a few spots left. To remind him that we had decided on this together—and to give him multiple chances to start doubting his decision—I updated Alon after completing each travel arrangement. It was ten days before the workshop and Alon was still cool as a cucumber.

One evening I said outright: "You realize we're going, don't you? If you're not into it, let's talk about it now, so that what happened to us in Guatemala doesn't happen again."

"Maybe we should tell our parents before making a final decision? It is Egypt after all," Alon suggested.

When I informed my mom that Alon and I were travelling to a sexuality workshop in Egypt, she replied with a straight face that she and my father were going to a yoga workshop in Syria. In other words, they were not thrilled with the idea. Neither were Alon's parents. They worried that despite Israel's peace treaty with Egypt, we wouldn't be safe there.

When we were alone, Alon suggested that we reconsider, or that I go without him.

I lost it. Because of our parents' reaction he wanted to back out? But I didn't insist this time. After one dramatic argument, I let Alon decide for himself whether he was truly interested in going. A few days later, probably because I let go, he decided he was.

THE NILE IS A CALM RIVER WITH NO WAVES. The boat was like a hotel floating on water. The cabins were spacious, decorated in brown and gold with wall-to-wall carpeting and wooden furniture. During the day we had a few group sessions in a room at the bottom of the boat and the rest of the time we spent on the deck. We sunbathed, read, and connected with the other participants. The situation was surreal and intense.

We sailed for a few hours each day, sitting on deck and passing the time. One day, Eliya, one of the organizers and a long-time member of the sexuality-studies community, came up to me and asked if I minded if she did one of the exercises with Alon. She expressed a desire to be intimate with him and exercises were the way to learn about both desire and intimacy.

"I'm really attracted to him and out of respect for you I wanted to ask you first," she said.

I thought her request didn't bother me.

"It's nice of you to ask," I said, surprisingly mature and non-possessive. "Yes. The communication that develops among the participants is so special…"

We continued to talk, sitting on the mat and cushions, holding hands in female solidarity, and while she started describing exactly what attracted her to Alon (she liked dark men and he was as beautiful as a Persian prince), I started to seethe. Not only was she attractive, and one of the workshop organizers—she was planning to make a move on him. Alon and I had already practiced with other people, but it had always been a one-off and in a setting that we could more or less control. I started imagining she and Alon spending all the breaks and doing all the exercises together; how from a trip that was supposed to connect us to my Yoni would become a pleasure cruise for my husband in which I was not aboard.

I kept my anger to myself. Slowly, I released my hand from hers and, still smiling, mumbled something about the bathroom and went down to see Alon in our room. Most of the crew members knew we had come on board for a sexuality workshop. In Egypt such a thing is unheard of, much less allowed. Moving between the practice space and the cabins, I often felt that the crew members were giving me a going-over.

Alon was lying in bed reading on his phone. Sitting down, I told him about the conversation with Eliya. It wasn't easy for me to see the smile spread across his face.

"What are you smiling about? Are you going to do anything about it?" I asked angrily.

Alon grabbed my waist, drew me closer and started kissing me. I kissed him back. We started pressing against each other while we took each other's clothes off. It suddenly occurred to me that maybe he was turned on by thinking about Eliya, and I was just an object for his fantasy. I moved away and onto my back. Alon got on top of me.

"Enough, I don't feel like it."

"A little more?" he kept going.

"We came here to focus on me!" I reminded him. "To learn about my pleasure, remember?" At those words, Alon lay on his back and let his hands fall to his side. By now I sounded like a broken record to both of us.

We turned our backs to each other and didn't speak for several minutes. We were in the middle of the Nile, stuck in a storm of our own making. At our usual loss. I looked at the clock and saw that it was almost 3:30.

"There's a session starting now," I told Alon and got up. He didn't respond. I was too afraid to ask if he was coming, because I really wanted him to. I changed into comfortable clothes and left the room—and the door open behind me.

As I reached the main hall at the bottom of the boat, I saw that Alon had entered. All the workshop participants were there, around 30 people, all standing. I walked over to John and Yael, friends of ours, and stood beside them. I was at an angle in which I could see both the facilitators' faces and Alon's. Alon stood at the opposite side of the room and avoided eye contact with me.

Today we are here to bless the Lingam, the facilitator explained. The women will kneel, visually behold their partner's Lingam, and bless it. This is not a sexual situation in which you seek to give pleasure, the focus is on blessing." He dimmed the lights.

I walked up to Alon and kneeled before him. I didn't care about the fight, I wanted to make clear that we were doing this exercise together, and under no circumstances with Eliya. We stood in couples, the women on their knees and the men naked in front of them. The men weren't in a position, physically or otherwise, of "come and serve us"; on the contrary: they were exposed, vulnerable and embarrassed. This situation allowed me to set aside my anger. Releasing the tension that had descended on us back in the room, I devoted myself to the exercise. I blessed Alon's Lingam. I noticed that Alon was still detached and angry, but I ignored it.

I spoke to his Lingam from the bottom of my heart: "You're strong. You're full of life. You're vital. You're significant. You're important. You're present. I want to be close to you." Alon shut his eyes tight and started to smile. Every few seconds he opened his eyes, looked at me with a loving expression, and caressed my face. I caressed him back.

For the first time I understood the cliché about "makeup sex." The best way to make up after a fight is through the body. If I had tried to appease him with words, we would have remained stuck. By giving so much love and respect to his sexual organ in an unconditional way, a new intimacy was created between me and Alon. We came out of that exercise as in love as if we had just met.

THAT WAS THE FIRST TIME WE HAD FOCUSED DIRECTLY ON THE SEXUAL ORGAN without foreplay or discussion. We experienced in the flesh how respecting each other's sexual organs, as well as our own, was the key to moving forward. The challenge now was to create a deeper connection to my Yoni. Both Alon and I were still detached from her. I couldn't really articulate what gave her pleasure, I didn't have a direct channel of communication with her, sometimes she still suddenly closed up or became wet, but in a way that felt unrelated to my experience. I felt as if she wasn't part of my body.

The next day the facilitators announced it was time to focus on the Yoni. They called her "The Temple" and invited us to participate in a ceremony called Yoni Gazing. Anyone who wanted to participate was invited to lie down on a mattress without underwear and with her legs spread wide. The men would walk among the participants and look at their Yoni. For the women, the goal was to be seen in a safe space, to dispel the shame surrounding our sexual organs that we had lived with for so long. For the men the goal was to look at the Yoni and show her respect and love without wanting anything in return. If the woman agreed, the man could offer feedback about what he saw between her legs, not as a grade or with adjectives, but by relating to certain qualities. "I can see it is sensitive, it reminds me of a flower, etc."

I survived for exactly four minutes. It was too much for me. I didn't know myself what my Yoni looked like, so it was strange for me to have someone else look at it. At the start of the exercise, Alon walked up to me and kissed me, even though it wasn't allowed, but the moment another man approached and stood there staring at my privates, that was it. I drew my legs in and sat out the rest.

I saw George, a gay man from the U.S., lingering by the Yoni of one of the participants and almost praying to her. At one point, he was so moved he cried. I saw another woman groaning in pleasure, pulling a man's finger and inserting it into her Yoni, also not following the instructions. I saw women with their legs spread and their head to one side, detached from the situation. Others had a big smile across their lips. One woman shed a few tears as she scanned the faces of all those who had paid homage to her Yoni.

Two amazing women from Israel, Rachel and Sivan, also participated in the workshop. It was the same Rachel who had facilitated one of Double You's Red Tent sessions. Rachel and Sivan were a couple at the time, although they both also had male lovers. When I saw how they completely devoted themselves to the exercise, I realized that some women have no issues with their Yoni, and that they could be our address to learn about mine. After the ceremony, I asked if, when we were back in Israel, they would join Alon and me in a session, and was thrilled when they agreed.

OUR LIVING ROOM IN JAFFA WAS A PLACE WHERE YOU COULD HOLD CEREMONIES. It had a high, five-meter ceiling, windows draped with red curtains and cushions spread out on the floor. The idea was that Rachel would give Sivan a Yoni massage while Alon gave me one, allowing Rachel to guide him in the process while having a view of both Yonis.

It was a winter day. When they arrived we drank tea, ate hummus and talked about what was going on in our lives. After we were sated and updated, we pushed some cushions together and spread a sheet over them. Rachel arranged some special stones in the room and explained that they emanated energy and offered blessings. Sivan and I scattered candles around and lit them. Alon put on some relaxing music.

We stood in a circle in the living room and held hands. Each one said what their intention was for that session. I said that mine was to get to know my Yoni and strengthen the trust between it and Alon. After we finished the round, we took our clothes off and danced a little to the music. After a few minutes, Sivan and I lay down on the cushions.

"We're going to be working on two levels here," Rachel said. "On the physical level, massaging the Yoni is massaging muscle tissue, like massaging tight muscles. You're familiar with this massage from the work you have already done together at the workshop. On the energy level, the Yoni is the source of the flow from the womb to the heart. She encapsulates all the trauma and injury that affects a woman's sexual behavior. The encounter with the Yoni is an opportunity for healing and holiness. When we are given permission to enter the Yoni, it's like entering a temple. Imagine that you're meditating or praying through your touch."

I was moved by Rachel's words, and was glad that Alon was hearing them. I smiled, closed my eyes and felt completely open to a transformative experience.

That is, until Alon started touching me. As always, it was too hard, and as always I reproached him.

"It hurts," I rasped. "Do it more gently, more slowly."

Alon stopped and gave me a downcast look.

Rachel could tell we were about to fight and intervened. "Imagine that you're touching like a feather," she said, "as gentle as you can imagine."

She demonstrated on Sivan. He watched, then imitated her movements on my Yoni.

"At first you just go around," instructed Rachel. "You don't touch directly. Look at the outer lips, the sides, one point after the other, remember the feather."

I managed to feel relaxed for a few minutes. I signaled to Alon he could enter. Alon immediately put his finger inside me. It was apparently too soon.

"Actually, not yet," I said and shot him a frown.

"Wait a minute," said Rachel. "We're in no hurry to get anywhere. See how I'm touching Sivan, and how her Yoni is slowly opening up like a flower."

I was jealous of Sivan. I also wanted to open up like a flower. I wanted someone like Rachel to open me. I was angry. I started moving uncomfortably and complaining about every move Alon made: "That's too strong. Not there. It hurts here."

By now Alon was angry too.

He removed his fingers and then sat hugging his knees. How many times had my comments closed the both of us up?

"Hang on," said Rachel, "this is the moment to work through your frustration. Feel empathy for her place. Imagine what it's like to be in her place, to have a Yoni, and how you constantly have to protect yourself from being entered, so that you don't get hurt."

We were silent but looked into each other's eyes.

"Feel empathy for his place too," said Rachel. "Imagine having to find your way around this mysterious thing called a Yoni, having to know how to touch it, and getting an earful every time you do."

We continued looking at each other. Tears came to our eyes. It was quiet. Alon reentered my Yoni with his fingers. It still hurt, but this time, instead of being angry, I inhaled deeply. Alon went on looking at me, he could tell I was in pain, stayed in the same spot, put his hand on my heart and invited me with his gaze to breathe.

I noticed that he was completely present and with each passing moment he became more and more gentle. The more I noticed it, the more I softened, opened up and felt love. Alon touched different spots in my Yoni, and wherever it hurt we stopped and breathed until the pain was replaced by pleasure. Alon was in me with his fingers for almost forty minutes, exploring my Yoni. I was no longer in pain and Alon was no longer paralyzed. Something flowed, flowered, between us, we laughed and cried together. At one point I completely lost my sense of time and identity. I had no thoughts, everything was flowing, like in a trance. When he touched my G-spot the pleasure was overwhelming. Usually I would stop at this point because I couldn't contain it. But now, the further I lost my orientation, the deeper the pleasure became. It was like the room had started spinning and I... came. For the first time I reached an orgasm with Alon.

Alon gazed into my eyes with a smile of relief. I gazed back, communicating that I was his. We hugged for several hours.

We don't usually cuddle in our sleep, because it keeps us awake, but that night we stayed locked in each other's arms. Each one of us held our heads a little higher, as if we had overcome the "failure" that shamed us each and every day.

IN THE PAST, I COULDN'T STAND HAVING MY CLITORIS TOUCHED. When Alon would try, I'd immediately move his hand away. That area was too sensitive for me. I couldn't understand the sensations I experienced when my clitoris was touched. Did it tickle? Hurt? Itch? I don't know. At the workshops we always avoided working on that.

A few weeks after our ceremony at home, when we were both already friendly with my Yoni, we signed up for a half-day workshop in Israel. There, we learned about the clitoris. I learned that the little piece of flesh visible to the eye is the peak of a vast mountain. Most of the clitoris is inside the body. The upper part is only the tip! They explained that we had thousands of nerve endings in it, double what men had, for the sole purpose of experiencing deep pleasure.

We had a Yoni ceremony, as we had done in previous workshops, but this time we were instructed to give the clitoris special attention. Alon started with a full body massage, moved on to the Yoni, and before entering it, approached the clitoris. Alon was on edge. He was used to me forbidding him from going anywhere near there. I tried to relax. I closed my eyes and focused on my heartbeat.

Next to Alon was our friend Gili. He had attended many sessions by Om, a center for orgasmic meditation in New York that taught men how to elicit a female orgasm. Gili whispered things into Alon's ear that I couldn't hear. When I opened my eyes for a moment, I saw him demonstrating in the air what Alon was supposed to do.

Alon started off with delicate caressing in very small parts on the clitoris I didn't even know existed. He made circles around it and then circles around the corners, and at one point I no longer knew what he was doing, and I started melting and connecting with the energy that entered every pore of my body. This energy wrapped me in a tingling cloak that endowed me with strength, capacity, the motivation to live. Layers upon layers of pleasure. It was the same energy we had in our previous session, but this time it came really fast. Surprised at what this region of the body is capable of, I burst into laughter, cried and shouted for joy. I opened my eyes. Alon and Gili were standing over me, overjoyed, beaming.

This is what peace among men and women looks like, I thought in ecstasy.

I once heard someone say that for wars to end, every man need only look into the eyes of a woman while she is giving birth. What would happen if men invested the energy required to learn how to touch a woman's clitoris?

After the session I was...empowered. There's no other word for it. I walked with my back straight, I was present. I felt as if I could do anything. Suddenly, I had discovered what hid behind the pleasure. It wasn't only satisfying needs or momentary urges. Behind pleasure resides a real force, a corporeal energy force, that can be used to implement action—to turn ideas into reality. I was exposed to a drive within me that I hadn't known existed.

That evening I was slated to present to the management team of a startup I had been consulting for. I felt at ease, and even more so afterwards. Any challenge to my plan was met with a creative solution that I had come up with on the spot. Things that would usually cause me to become defensive or argumentative, when someone didn't agree with one of my ideas, did not set me off. I was more efficient. For how many years had I underestimated the potential of the clitoris? People take drugs to boost confidence, but so much of what we need is naturally available in our very own bodies.

The clitoris is a gateway for women to power and knowledge. It teaches a woman what pleasure is, and that pleasure can be a compass to lead us toward life's milestones, and away from the things not worth pursuing. The mental image I had during that exercise was of a sexual energy that fills our body and becomes a part of us. We have to make room to let it in, and assimilate it into our lives. At that session, when I reached an orgasm so quickly, it wasn't easy to contain the pleasure.

GILI AND ALON TOLD ME THAT AT THE HEIGHT OF THE SESSION, while laughing in delight, I also curled up and hid. Physically, my legs folded inward and my hands covered my face.

"Spread your hands out, take pride in your pleasure," they encouraged me during the exercise. I tried but I was embarrassed, maybe even ashamed. I was experiencing a new force and it would take me time to navigate it.

In the three years studying sexuality, we kept going one step forward and then, as we returned to our daily lives, two steps back. This time we connected to my Yoni in a transformative way, and there was no turning back. Our sexual connection was unquestionable. It was clear that now we knew how to generate sexual fulfillment. We still had challenges, but we knew how to handle them.

Our sexual encounters became exciting, diverse and rich. From one encounter to the next the interaction became more complex. Alon would explore the folds of my Yoni with his fingers as if walking in his childhood neighborhood: knowing what opens, challenges, softens and what makes her blush. Every time Alon knew my Yoni in this way, I became even more familiar with her, and that opened my heart to him like never before.

As always, I saw the impact this change had on my professional life. The more I loved Alon and delved deeper into pleasure, the more I wanted to invest in our work with the women at Double You, and take bolder steps.

At the time, most of my energy was focused on consulting startups and organizations, which was how I made a living. Double You was a workshop that took place annually or biannually, boasting almost 1,000 participants over the years. However, since the companies I was consulting were financially stable, I considered my work with them to be my "real" job, and dedicated most of my time to it.

Right about then, I had the first real opportunity to use my Companion ticket. A few months earlier, I had started working with a well-funded Jewish organization that operated international leadership networks for adults and teenagers in Europe, America and Israel. They hired me to lead processes with their team of guides, including group dynamics, entrepreneurial thinking and brainstorming. The first time I worked with them was in Israel, with delegations from their teams. Now I had received an invitation directly from Eitan, the CEO himself, to travel to Chicago and present an adapted version of the workshop to the management team.

The organization employed hundreds of employees and Eitan was a very idealistic man, everyone's pal, a person you couldn't help being enchanted by. I met him at a social entrepreneurs' dinner a few years earlier, where he described how his organization was changing American-Israeli relations through summer camps for Jewish youth.

When he spoke, all I wanted to do was join the mission he was leading. I was impressed by his ability to think on a grand scale, how he wasn't shy about selling or asking for the resources he needed, and by the way he connected to each person and made them feel special.

We clicked at once. He said I was a bulldozer, and sharp as a needle, and that he would be happy if we could join forces. I was thrilled by the prospect of working together, and wanted to be, put to the test, to see for the first time how I would conduct myself with men in the professional world.

When I started working with Eitan's organization, most of my work wasn't directly with him, but once a month we would speak and catch up, and these talks gave me a huge boost. He was one of those people who made me want to be better at what I was doing, and every good word from him spurred me on.

This time I brought along a colleague, Dorit, who was versed in consulting large corporations in Europe in the fields of organizational culture and creating communities. Dorit thrived on work, meeting new people and adventure. When we started planning the presentation, I noticed that she was thinking mostly about the employees' experience while I was thinking mostly about Eitan.

EITAN PREFERRED UNIQUE WORKSHOPS PRESENTED IN AN "OUT OF THE BOX" MANNER, and I liked living up to his expectations. We had two weeks to prepare for the workshop we would be giving to his team. Dorit and I spent days and nights shaping everything to be more suited to management. Dorit took a normal flight while I had my secret Companion arrangement. The disadvantage was that to get anywhere I had to fly through Barcelona, London or New York, because the airline had no direct flights from Israel.

I joined the stand-by list for a few relevant flights. I didn't know how long it would take me to find a seat on a connecting flight to Barcelona, so I took an extra day to be on the safe side. At the airport I showed the receptionist my confirmation. She signaled to me to stand aside and wait. An hour later I reminded her of my existence. Checking the screen, she said there was a spot.

"In business?" I asked in childlike excitement. It was the first facial expression I received from her. A half-smile.

"Sweetie, the flight is fully-booked," she said. "You've got a seat in the second-to-last row in the middle. You should be thankful that you're even boarding the flight."

In Barcelona the same thing happened all over again. When I spoke to the ground attendants I worried that they would ask about my relationship with the airline employee, because I wouldn't be able to lie.

From New York, I had one flight to go. I checked which ones were available. Taking the first two flights had been exciting, but by now I had gotten the idea. I was exhausted from being up in the air for so long and the covert operation I was a part of. I slept for the three-hour duration of the flight, waking up only when the captain announced: "Welcome to Chicago."

Dorit and I met at the hotel, in the room we were sharing. I felt such relief at seeing a familiar face. We hugged, rehearsed our presentation and walked around town.

I SENT EITAN A MESSAGE: "I'M HERE. You can't imagine what an amazing program we've prepared for you! Excited about tomorrow." A while later I saw two blue ticks, but no reply.

The next day the workshop took place in the hotel conference room. It was full of people I didn't recognize. I didn't see Eitan. The management team looked very different from the organization's guides. They were in suits, their heads buried in their laptops, and the atmosphere was charged. Giving Dorit and myself a quick going-over, I wondered if we had dressed for the occasion.

"Are you Narkis?" someone I didn't know asked me in English.

"Yes," I replied. "And this is Dorit."

"I'm Eitan's assistant. Welcome. How was your flight? "

"Flights," I clarified.

"Sorry?"

"Never mind. It was fine. How are you? And why is the atmosphere so tense? I've met your guides in Israel several times and they were more relaxed. We've prepared some exercises that will require people to leave their comfort zones and I just want to make sure it's suitable for this crowd," I said.

"The team here is made up of former guides. Everyone is usually pretty easygoing. It's just that you've arrived before the board meeting where everyone has to get their annual plans approved, so they have to finalize their budgets and goals. It's usually much more upbeat around here." The assistant smiled.

"I hope they have the patience for our group dynamics exercises," I said, still concerned.

"Would you like something to drink? Coffee helps against worries," she replied, still smiling.

"It's OK. We'll be fine. Thanks!"

Dorit and I went over everything again, deciding to leave out two activities. Then I gave Dorit and myself a pep talk: "It will be fine. Let's just do it the way we practiced. It will change the energy in the room," I cheered each other on.

Dorit smiled and replied: "Remember, no matter what happens — we did our very best."

OK, I thought to myself, that's not very reassuring.

I stood up in front of everyone, the presentation already on the screen. Eitan walked into the room. I smiled at him. He stood beside us, hugged me and shook Dorit's hand. Then he introduced us: "Narkis has worked with our teams of guides in Israel. She brings with her Israeli hutzpah and the ability to think outside the box, which is just what I'd like our organizational culture to adopt. That's why I have invited Narkis and..."

"Dorit," I said and he went on. "—Yes, to come here and conduct a group dynamics workshop and present brainstorming methodologies that will encourage innovative entrepreneurial thinking. Enjoy," he smiled and left the room. I was shocked. Where was he going? What about our presentation? I tried to rein in my disappointment.

I usually started off workshops with an anecdote that would draw people in, and had dedicated a lot of thought into choosing the right story for this organization's mission. I decided to share how being in a youth movement had changed my life. While I was speaking, half the people in the room were fiddling with their phones. I went on for a few more minutes, trying to ignore it, but with every passing moment it seemed like I was losing another member of the audience. I glanced at Dorit, who gave me a small smile of support.

After fifteen minutes that felt like an eternity, Dorit came up to do her part. I walked over to Eitan's assistant.

"Where did he go?" I asked.

"He's also presenting his annual plan this week. He has important calls with donors," she explained.

"Can you take me to him for a second? I'd like to talk to him."

"He's right in the middle of the calls."

"Yes, I understand, but part of the team isn't attentive and as long as he isn't present to show them that it's important, that won't change. You'll just be wasting your money."

"The team actually seems very attentive. The fact that he organized this workshop during such a hectic a week conveys just how important it is. And the fact that he's not here actually shows the team that he really trusts you. He doesn't do this with everyone."

"So you can also trust me — he needs to be here. Take me to him, please."

She led me out of the workshop room and pointed to a door. I walked in and Eitan signaled that he would be with me in a sec.

"Eitan, come. It's really important that you be there," I said. "Otherwise, it won't work."

He put the call on mute and said, "I'm sorry, I'm in the middle of some really important calls. Is everything OK?"

"We just need you in the room with us."

"OK, I'll come when I can," he said and went back to the call.

"Please come, it's important to me," I pleaded.

Already back on his call, Eitan signaled "soon" again with his hand.

I felt like I did when I was a little girl and my father was working in his study and I'd ask him to stop and come play with me; or when I had a crush on my youth group leader, who barely found a spare second to say hi to me; or when I worked at a startup and my boss managed the meetings, paying attention to all the VPs while not giving me the time of day.

I returned to the workshop with my tail between my legs and spent the remaining hour in an internal struggle. In the last two minutes of our presentation, Eitan stepped into the room and sat down.

WHEN WE WERE DONE, EITAN CLAPPED LOUDLY AND THE OTHERS JOINED HIM. "Thank you, well done, thank you very much!" He stood up before the crowd, thanked us again and smiled at me. I gave him a half-smile back. My body was wracked with insult. All the times I had worshiped men who didn't pay attention to me constricted my throat, and I had to keep myself from crying. Dorit tried to make eye contact, but to no avail. Back in the hotel room we tried a post mortem.

"I feel terrible," I told Dorit. "What a disaster. We couldn't have been worse."

"You're exaggerating a little," she replied. "I agree that it wasn't amazing, but it wasn't terrible."

"What are you talking about? Half of them were on their phones and the others were indifferent to our exercises."

"It's true, some were on their phones — that's what happen when you give a workshop in the middle of a workday. But some showed interest and you never know how something you said might influence people later on."

"Influence people? Eitan wasn't even in the room!"

"Narkis... the workshop was for the management team, not the CEO."

"Yes, but if it was really important he would have been there."

"Not necessarily. It's because it was important that he invited us. We came here to help his managers. Why was it so important to you that he be there?"

"For his feedback. He's the one running the organization."

"OK… Let's wait for the feedback forms," said Dorit with a judgmental expression, as if she could see something I couldn't. It annoyed me. I told myself that she didn't have enough experience consulting for startups, that she didn't realize just how imperative the relationship with the CEO was. At night, replaying everything that had gone down on this terrible day, I had a hard time falling asleep.

The next day, after the workshops with the other teams, an unpleasant truth was revealed: there had been nothing wrong with Eitan's conduct. He was just doing his work as a CEO who was busy fundraising for the organization he was running. But the organization wasn't what really interested me. It could just as well have been a business selling car tires, and I'd still come to give the workshops.

The managers' behavior the previous day reflected my own attitude: some of them ignored me because they felt they were being ignored. The only thing I cared about in this gig was getting Eitan's attention. There was nothing romantic, sexual or even personal about it. It was something else.

On that trip I realized that my work with organizations and startups always revolved around one variable: my rapport with the CEOs. The common denominator was that both were successful, smart, and doted on me. Which mirrored my relationship with my father.

MY FATHER IS ONE OF THE TOP MATHEMATICIANS IN HIS FIELD. When I was young, I didn't know how successful he was. I remember the day it dawned on me — I was in the third grade and he was helping me with my math homework. After a few minutes of him explaining something I couldn't make heads or tails of, I lost my patience and threw my pencil onto the floor: "I don't feel like doing homework!" I shouted. "I'm leaving!"

"Wait, stay," he asked. "I want you to understand, it's important that you understand, this is the basis of math."

"So? And if I don't understand the basis of math? You're not the smartest person in the world either!"

Calmly, my father said: "Some actually might say I am."

My mouth opened wide but I said nothing.

A few years ago I met a well-known entrepreneur who had made an exit with a VR technology company. At the meeting I suggested that each one say something about themselves. He began by saying that he had studied math and physics. At that detail, I interrupted him and said proudly, "My father is a mathematician."

"Yes, I know who your father is," he replied. "He's my favorite mathematician in Israel, and you're his daughter and I love you."

It wasn't the first time a stranger had expressed love, appreciation and respect for me just for being my father's daughter.

I'm similar to my father in many ways. For starters, we're both competitive and ambitious. In the past, our conversations often revolved around achievements. I'd ask him about the prizes he had won and those he had yet to win, and he would ask me about my grades and offer tips for getting better ones. I always felt that the more successful I was, the more I would be loved and the more attention I would get, particularly from smart men.

When I meet a smart and successful man, he interests me not romantically, but intellectually. I immediately start up a conversation, hoping he'll want to work together, hoping he'll think I'm smart, too. I bring up topics I think he would appreciate, and take them as far as I can go.

When it doesn't work, it hurts. With my father it almost never worked because he never wanted me to try to impress him is his field; rather, he wanted me to be the best in whatever interested me.

I remember, when I was seventeen, sitting in the living room and watching TV. There was a news item about the people helping develop a new drug for Teva Pharmaceuticals. They presented each person, the drug's sales figures, and how many jobs it had created. Afterwards, I turned off the TV and continued staring at the dark screen.

My father sat down on the couch next to me and asked, "What's up?"

"I have an idea," I said. "I'll study chemistry at the university, then go for an advanced degree and work hard to get good grades. Along the way I'll get to know people and after we graduate we'll apply for internships at places like Teva. There, in the lab, we'll conduct tons of experiments until we come up with a new medicine."

"Where is all this coming from?" my father asked. I had spent most of my time in the Scouts until then and never showed any interest in science.

I turned to him. "I just saw something about a team that made a lot of money doing that and made a real impact. The world of health is important, and it's also a real science, isn't it?" Dad said about any field that wasn't an exact science that it wasn't a science. Psychology wasn't a science, sociology wasn't a science, and even statistics.

"It's better to focus on areas you're really interested in," he said with affection. "If you chase money it's no fun. Do what's fun and interesting regardless of what you receive in return. You'll have a fulfilling life that way." He smiled, put his hand on my shoulder and went back to work. It took a few years for the message to sink in. It was only when I started following his advice and walking my own path that I started seeing my father for who he is: a dedicated and talented man doing the same.

From the moment I stopped trying to imitate him and became my own person, we grew closer. We had shared topics that could develop into real conversations. The things I had chosen to focus on were not only not related to my father, until today he doesn't fully understand what they're all about. When his friends ask him what I do, he says: "I can't really explain, something to do with social projects and women, but I know she's happy and thriving."

BUT AT THE END OF THE TRIP TO THE STATES I felt like a failure. On the last evening, after we finished giving all the workshops, Dorit and I drove to the airport and said goodbye. Dorit was taking a normal flight that would depart in two hours, and I had to figure out which flight would let me on it and wear my poker face while talking to the ground attendants.

I was tired and my legs itched. I joined the stand-by lists of a few flights with available seats, then spent the next hour on a different mission: finding some aloe vera to soothe my itch. All I could find after scouring the airport was body cream, which I slathered on my legs shamelessly right outside the store.

On the screen I saw there was room on a flight leaving in two hours — my route was Chicago-Newark-London. There I would have to catch another flight. I would reach Israel in 32 hours at best.

On the trans-Atlantic flight between Newark and London, I pushed my first class seat all the way back and tried to get some shut-eye. I had had a sleepless night, but I couldn't fall asleep. I was so itchy. At one point I took my pants off and remained in my underwear under the blanket, trying not to scratch.

Negative thoughts pursued me. On flights I would usually sail to faraway places and dream up grand visions about my future, but now I was capsizing.

From my playlist I put on the song "Illusions" by Nissim Sarussi: "Living in a luxury apartment, thinking that you're a millionaire… Never work, never serve anyone, your head high in the clouds, climbing up — you are living illusions!"

I couldn't listen to another word. How detached I was from reality! I thought about all the times I explained my work to people, presenting my consultation service as something groundbreaking, as if I was leading some mega movement that was spreading the principles of female leadership across world organizations.

In reality, I presented some workshops to multiple organizations. In the process, I mostly sought out the attention of the CEOs, a full-time job that took so much out of me, I neglected my work with the women in Double You—which was why I had set out on this journey to begin with. At one point, after hours of self-flagellation and leg-scratching, I fell asleep.

I landed in London a total wreck, only to discover that I had to wait four more hours for an available flight. This was the last time I would travel with such a god-awful Companion. I should have listened to Alon.

I sent Erik a message: "Remember what we agreed on? It's not working out. You promised you'd reimburse me $3,500, please wire it over." It took three months and a slew of messages, and even then, he only paid back $2,000.

I paid back the remaining $5,000 to our joint account, in installments. In tears I admitted to Alon that he had been right. He went easy on me, only saying that if it was too hard, I didn't have to pay it all back, but that was not an option for me — I had given my word and reimbursed him to the last dollar. Until then, that was the most expensive mistake I had ever made.

When I returned from the trip I made some decisions: I would step it up at Double You and cut down on the projects that didn't advance the same vision; I would write a talk about women and sexuality; I would think about starting a family. I sent out applications to lecture at a few conferences and broached the subject of kids with Alon. I wanted to be a mom. We had released so many sexual blockages between us, and I had always considered pregnancy and birth as the highest fulfillment of sexuality.

A month later Alon was ready to start trying. I was getting back on the right track and decided that if there was a business trip or conference that Alon chose not to join me on, I wouldn't go. I had done my part — now it was time for the universe to do hers.

CHAPTER 5
TEACH ME HOW TO BECOME A STRONG WOMAN

"One is not born, but rather becomes a woman."

Simone de Beauvoir

WE MANAGE DOUBLE YOU AS A GROUP. At this point we are already eight partners. Any decision regarding content, community management or distribution of funds has to be harmoniously agreed on. Most of the time it goes smoothly, but occasionally differences of opinion, ego clashes, insults and even jealousy break out. Unlike regular organizations, where such occurrences are suppressed or ignored, with us everything is on the table. In the past, when there were such tensions among team members, my tendency was to call it quits.

I can't pinpoint the exact moment it occurred, but somewhere along the way I decided that my partners and my relationships with them were part of my life. It reminded me of a wedding I attended, where the groom told the bride that he had long since substituted the question "Is this relationship working?" with "What needs to be done to make this relationship go on working?"

Every management meeting starts with a sharing circle, where each participant shares how she is doing. It isn't uncommon for someone to cry at these meetings, out of excitement or while verbalizing her fears, dreams or request for help.

Then we move on to the tasks at hand. At one point, we get distracted and the conversation transitions to bursts of laughter: we laugh at ourselves or at those next to us, or simply break into a laughing fit, for no apparent reason. No matter in what condition I arrive at the meeting, there is always a point at which my heart opens and the liquids of love in my body cleanse my mind and soul. Love and friendship are the backbone of our team. It is for their sake that we dedicate so much of our time, and they are what protect us when we work on sensitive topics such as sexuality, personal crises and supporting Double You's women through mental and financial setbacks.

One day, during the period that Alon and I were trying to get pregnant, we had our monthly Double You meeting. We went over our annual plan and distributed tasks. When we came to the subject of a retreat slated to take place ten months from then, Stephie said she wouldn't be able to make it, and smiled.

"Why?" I asked.

"Because it will be after I give birth."

"You're pregnant?" asked Sarah.

"I think so, but I haven't checked yet."

"So how do you know?" I asked.

"I feel it," she replied confidently.

Maybe I was also pregnant? I wondered. On the way back from the meeting I stopped by the drugstore and bought two pregnancy tests. They both came out positive. According to our calculations, it looked like we were five weeks pregnant. We were beyond surprised. How could it have worked on our first try? Were we even ready for this? After we felt more at ease with the idea, the excitement set in. I spoke with all of my friends who were already mothers, asked a ton of questions, scoured everything I could online and made an appointment with an OBGYN.

At eight weeks, I went to the doctor with my two sisters, Nilli and Natalie. They were both mothers and my best friends. Just before we entered the room, Natalie stopped me and said, "I have a present for you." She took a book out of her bag called Nine Months.

"It's a funny and informative book that tells you what's happening in your body each week. I read it throughout my pregnancy." I hugged her and we walked in.

"These are my sisters," I said to the doctor by way of introduction.

"You've brought your two sisters to your first examination? That's a first," replied the doctor and smiled.

As he performed a vaginal ultrasound, he looked at the screen uncomfortably.

"What's the matter?" I asked.

"I felt your womb, you are pregnant, but I didn't expect the pregnancy sac to look like that," he said. "It might be a week earlier than we thought, and if that's the case then everything is OK. But if not then it might be an unviable pregnancy. I'd like to send you for some checkups this week to see what the situation is."

When we left Natalie took the book back and said, "I'll give it to you when we know you're pregnant for sure." Sheesh, I thought, why is everyone making such a fuss? I tried to think about manifesting reality. I imagined myself giving birth to a healthy child and believed that everything would be fine.

That night I slept soundly, and woke up in a good mood. At the women's health center, I had a blood and urine test. A few hours later I received the results: the hCG levels were dropping. Not a good sign.

I didn't want to call my gynecologist because I knew he would say that the test results suggested the pregnancy wasn't viable. I called my sisters' gynecologist, introduced myself, told her who my doctor was and which tests I had done that day. When I told her about the declining beta-hCG levels, she said that my pregnancy was definitely unviable. But I wouldn't give up. "Maybe I have twins and one of them died and that's why the levels have dropped?"

"No."

"Maybe my beta levels develop more slowly?"

"No, with the numbers you gave me it's certain."

"Maybe I should come in just to make sure."

"If you come in I'll just say the same thing — this pregnancy is unviable."

"But I want you to take a look on the monitor! I'll come right over, just take a look…" I wept.

"There's no need for you to come," she repeated.

"Make me an appointment! Please!" I went on crying and shouting at her, at this doctor I didn't know. Finally, she lost her calm and shouted back at me, "There's no reason for you to come see me, you have an excellent doctor — go see him! This pregnancy is unviable."

I was quiet for a long while.

"I'm sorry," she added. "I know it's hard."

THE NEXT DAY WE STARTED MAKING ARRANGEMENTS FOR THE ABORTION. It would involve pills to induce a miscarriage. We needed to complete the process because a week later Alon and I were flying together to the States. I was invited to speak about feminine leadership at a conference at Harvard and our plan was to take advantage of the ticket and fly on to Arizona to participate in a sex therapist training workshop.

We went to the medical center to do another hCG test and pick up the pills. Alon was clearly tense about work. He spent most of the time replying to emails and barely paid me any attention.

I was angry. I had to make a huge effort to make him understand that this was a matter that concerned both of us. On top of the feelings of shame and failure, something very significant had occurred in my body and I was experiencing grief. It wasn't rational. After all, it was only cells that hadn't developed into an embryo, but it brought up difficult emotions.

A week after the diagnosis, on Passover Eve, I had contractions and bleeding. There hadn't been a need for the pills — I was miscarrying. For days I bled and was in intense pain. Since there were no women who had a miscarriage in my close circle, I found myself reading posts online by women who shared what they had been through. One was a doula, who viewed miscarriage as an opportunity: "Many women when their body starts changing don't understand what's happening and, as a result, distance themselves from their bodies. Much like a girl who gets her first period and is disgusted by the process instead of understanding it, a woman who becomes pregnant and one who has a miscarriage share similar experiences. But every change is an opportunity to look within and come out stronger, more connected to the body. This connection prepares you for life, motherhood, femininity."

The post reminded me of the difficulties I had experienced during sex, which motivated me to embark on a sexuality learning journey. Could it be that a new journey awaited me? I wanted to accept what my body was going through, surrender myself to its movement, connect to my intuition, listen to signs. While I had these thoughts, Sound Cloud switched to the next song on my playlist, which repeated the words "Mother Ayahuasca" in Portuguese over and over again.

I FIRST HEARD OF AYAHUASCA WHEN I WAS 22 and, although I don't use drugs, I knew that I would try it one day. Ayahuasca is a vine that grows in the jungles of South America and is used, along with a plant from the coffee family that contains a psychoactive substance, to produce a brew. The combination of plants creates a prolonged hallucinatory state. The potion is mostly used in religious shaman ceremonies and in recent years has become popular among Westerners seeking a psychedelic experience.

Many people view Ayahuasca not as a drug but a medicine, an elevated entity which is described as a healing feminine presence. Many even call it "Grandma." Every person has a different experience with Ayahuasca. I have heard people describe visions related to nature, animals, angels and demons. While that song was playing, I thought: maybe it's time for me to meet Grandma?

After the miscarriage I felt confused, sad and that I had nothing to lose. What could happen? We were going to America and had a few days in between the conference and the workshop, and I might get pregnant again soon, after which it would no longer be possible.

I immediately called Yaniv, a good friend who had used his real estate savvy to partner up and buy an ecological mountain in Florianopolis, Brazil. There he founded an empowerment center with courses and workshops that combined self-development, community development, and connecting with nature. He named the place "Rosemary."

"I have a somewhat strange question," I said to Yaniv, with whom I hadn't spoken for a few months. "In two days I'm flying to the States. If we come visit you in Brazil, would you have any way of arranging an Ayahuasca ceremony for us?"

"Yes," he immediately replied.

"That was quick. Have you ever done it?" I asked.

"No, but if Alon and you are coming, I'll join you."

"I'm not sure Alon will want to or if it's even possible to change our plans, but I wanted to check with you first."

"From my end it's all open. I know a great shaman in the area. If you give me the exact dates I can coordinate it with him."

"Great, I'll get back to you soon." I hung up and smiled to myself. I tried to imagine who this shaman was, this person who knows how to communicate with the "world beyond" and guides journeys such as these. I understood from friends that who leads the ceremony is important.

When Alon returned to the room I laid my idea on him. "What do you say that instead of travelling around Arizona before the workshop, we visit Yaniv in Brazil?"

"I say that I love Yaniv and that nothing in the world would be more fun and that we don't have time," Alon quipped.

"We have five days after the conference in Boston, and I've checked the flights."

"We finally go to Brazil only to spend five days there? What will we manage to do in five days?"

"We'll see the business Yaniv built there and... do Ayahuasca."

"What? Where did this come from?" Alon smiled.

"It's been my dream for years," I said. "I really want to and I feel this is my time before the next pregnancy. It's a crazy idea, I know. But we'll be in America anyway. If you prefer, I'll go by myself, but we'd both have a good time at his place and the ceremony is just one evening."

Alon sat down next to me on the bed. He was wearing jeans and a T-shirt and I was in a robe and granny undies with pad, bleeding my miscarriage. He kissed me on the cheek, stroked my face, placed his hand on my contracting womb and said: "Let's do it."

FLORIANOPOLIS, BRAZIL. I'm lying on a bed at the Rosemary Center, a thin sheet covering me. A mosquito net hangs overhead, protecting me from the cloud buzzing around the room. We'll be leaving for the ceremony in twenty minutes, the four of us: me, Alon, Yaniv and a friend of his. One of my friends recommended remaining silent before the ceremony, and that I fast and concentrate on my intentions and the questions I'd like to ask.

Deviating from her recommendation, I ate fries at lunchtime, talked up a storm, and my thoughts were all over the place, rather than on the ceremony which, to be honest, really scared me. In the few minutes remaining before we got going, I jotted down a few things that I hoped to gain from the experience.

I wanted to connect to that inner voice that knows the way, the voice that understands what I'm meant to do in life. I wanted to meet this entity Ayahuasca, which everyone talks about, and ask her the following questions:

1. What is my mission in life?
2. Why did we have to go through the miscarriage?
3. When should we have children?
4. Am I headed in the right direction professionally?

Time to get ready.

The four of us met at Rosemary and shared a taxi into the village, half an hour away. When we arrived, Yaniv showed us the huge yurt where the ceremony was going to take place. For a few grueling minutes we climbed up the steep slope, at the top of which Erin the shaman was waiting. When I saw him I relaxed. He was young, with dreadlocks, and looked like someone who could be part of our group.

Erin introduced us to two other people who would be assisting him that evening. One had dark hair and rings in her ears, eyebrow, nose and tongue. She was quiet and avoided eye contact. I wondered whether she might be Erin's girlfriend, but didn't ask. The other guy had short black hair, brown eyes, a checkered shirt and *sharwal* pants. In the center of the yurt were musical instruments and against the walls, four mattresses with a yellow bucket next to each.

"What's the bucket for?" I asked.

"Your vomit," replied Erin. "Many people have a hard time absorbing the medicine at first. Emptying your stomach is part of the body's cleansing process."

Clearly this experience was going to take me far outside my comfort zone.

Erin sat us in a circle and said: "Ayahuasca is a medicine that has powers not of this world. She will affect you as much as you let her. If you surrender yourselves, she will do far-reaching work, and if you maintain your control, the experience you have will be mild. It's your choice. Your brain will feel different to you afterwards. Even if you're afraid that it will never be what it once was — don't worry, everything you feel will come to pass. Remember this during any difficult moments. We will drink a few rounds, one or more of which you may decide to forgo. Focus on 'your purpose' at all times," he said in his Portuguese accent, which made it sound like *propose*. "In between we will move among you, support you and play music. The music is an important part of the journey — it will help you surrender yourselves. Does anyone have any questions?"

We all wanted to get started at once.

Erin reduced the light in the yurt and instructed us to concentrate on the intention we had come with to the ceremony. Each of us walked up to the edge of the yurt and drank half a glass. The amount seemed too little to have any effect on my consciousness, but I told myself there would be more glasses. I drank, went back to the mattress and closed my eyes.

Nothing happened. What if I didn't feel anything all night? I had heard of people who had that experience. Erin was leading another ceremony this week, so I could always come and try again. I further worried that maybe I'd be one of those people who had a bad trip and saw demons and ghosts all night. I was on guard, waiting for monsters to appear, and every movement in the yurt made me flinch.

I don't know how much time passed before Erin called us for the second glass. When it was my turn he asked: "Do you feel anything?"

"No," I replied.

He smiled and gave me a fuller glass. I went back to the mattress and closed my eyes. Now something was stirring. My body became lighter, but not in a way that I hadn't already experienced through meditation and lucid dreaming. When Erin suggested a third and final glass, I jumped at the opportunity and asked for a full one.

I returned to the mattress; before I knew it, I had lost interest in my surroundings and started to go deeper and deeper into myself. Any fears completely dissolved. I remember going to the bathroom and seeing Alon on the way. We stared deep into each other's eyes. Alon looked at me with a combined half-smile and elusive gravity. We were both in our own worlds and about to leap into the rabbit's hole, each on our own journey.

I returned and surrendered myself. I started speaking to the Ayahuasca being, the way religious people speak to God. I yearned to meet her. "I want to get to know you"; "Show me your powers. Teach me how to become a strong woman"; "I want to feel what it's like to be part of you." All sentences that came from a hidden place inside me.

A great presence of power consumed my consciousness and body. I moved my mouth in slow motion, as if about to swallow something, as if I was a lion. I waved my hands in all directions, as if I was flying through the air. I felt pleasure, as if I was experiencing an orgasm, and even started to groan. In between moans, I repeated this sentence hundreds of times: "I love you, Ayahuasca, I'll do anything for you." I felt it fully, I shouted and screamed it. I watched my body and consciousness completely surrender themselves. It was if I had pleaded: "Take me, Ayahuasca, I sacrifice myself to you."

In a frenzy, I danced in celebration of Ayahuasca. My whole body produced a whole range of pleasurable sounds. I was in a trance, losing my identity and becoming part of Ayahuasca and what she represented: a net of femininity derived from the earth, animalism, and complete surrender. I saw geometric shapes that formed and merged together, all belonging to something greater, and I was an inseparable part of this source, which was everything.

In that vision I understood something about power and influence — there is another dimension of reality. What we see in the physical world is just the very tip of what underlies existence. In my vision, everyone worshiped this power that the Ayahuasca represented. Everyone was addicted and bowed down to her. I saw famous people in my vision: Beyoncé, Erik Schmidt, world leaders, and they were all like dogs with their tongues hanging out, wanting nothing but to take part in the power she represents. That was their only true end, and their actions and presence on Earth merely a means to that end. And we lowly people? We worshipped these characters and wanted a speck of their power for ourselves, but they didn't even care about that. They were busy worshiping the hidden powers of the great goddess, the animal lying deep in the ground, and wanted every piece of the love and pleasure she could give..

In that state, the physical world suddenly seemed boring to me, like child's play, no more than an act. I groaned to Ayahuasca, "I'll do anything for you, I'll bring you to the masses, I will teach about you," as my frenzied celebration—this vision of mine— became ever more intense.

At one point I remembered the questions I had, but when I started asking them — when to have children and how to make a living — it was obvious that if I belong to her, I had everything. It was as if she was saying: "It doesn't matter. Become whoever you want; learn to integrate me and expand what I represent." I remember myself telling her, "It's such luck that my partner is meeting you now too. I could never be with someone who hadn't met you, because you are the essence of my world."

The moment I merged with her completely was the moment I really became hers, as I had asked—became integrated into particles and geometric shapes that I had seen. I was no longer a separate being named Narkis, I was part of a whole, and there was no turning back. At this point, the experience stopped being positive.

Most people who take Ayahuasca close their eyes and behold visions, but when they open them again they see a normal room and realize they are in a ceremony. My experience was of totality. I was certain that what I saw in the vision was the world, and that all there was in it was all there would ever be. The world became a place in which everyone merged, everyone was one. Anything I envisioned could materialize in a split-second, and I could be everywhere at once. I remember thinking, "Omnipotence. This ability to be everything, any place and any time, represents the height of intelligence. But if this is the pinnacle, where are we rushing?"

What had first pulled me in now pushed me out. It seemed as if energy was passing too fast from place to place without a grounded event that allowed me to truly experience it. I became abstract in an abstract world where everything was part of a whole.

There were no more distinct people in the world with distinct experiences, no relationships between people, no relation at all.

At this point I realized I was cut off from all the people I knew and loved — my parents, Alon, Yaniv, my niece and nephew, my sisters, Sarah — in this world none of them existed. It wasn't clear whether they knew it or were just about to discover that they had come to populate this abstract world. It was like the matrix had exploded. Some probably knew. Now it was my turn to find out. But was that it? Gone were my human experiences? I felt great sadness, even terror, and there was nothing I could do about it.

I remembered what the shaman had said at the start of the ceremony, that our brain would feel changed and it would pass, but those words were empty now; he had known that after drinking Ayahuasca there was going back, and now we were trapped in this world of "truth."

While plagued by these thoughts and fears, I still groaned. I couldn't help it. I was hers. She was pressing on my neural pleasure centers and enslaving me to her. I remembered a quote from the Baal Shem Tov, "constant pleasure is no pleasure." That was an understatement; constant pleasure was Hell on Earth.

In a sense, it was the end of the world as we know it, a vision that various spiritual theories ascribe to — we were all created from a divine spark and one day will return to it. I had entered into a space where we had no identity, will, or form; we were pure consciousness. But rather than partaking in the process of creation, we were pawns of it, just like in The Matrix — our energy was being exploited.

I asked myself: How did this happen? How did humanity come to this? After a few hours of seeing nothing but geometrical figures, my consciousness started presenting me with images. I saw Facebook's Mark Zuckerberg and Sheryl Sandberg. I realized that Facebook was the first to persuade us to renounce our identity, the more we exposed it on social media. This virtual existence created by these networks is detached from our body and the physical world, and will ultimately cut us off from our very selves.

The second image was of Louharya, the spiritual teacher I had studied with in an organization called the Cosmic University. Seeing her and someone from her team, I asked them what happened, where humanity had disappeared to. They replied that we had discussed this very development in class, and knew that humanity was destined to return to a divine union. And that we must accept it with peace and love.

But I couldn't. There were still so many things I wanted to experience in the normal world, as a human being. I remembered some of the friends I had, who used to say that there is so much suffering in the world, and that they would be happy to die and unite with the spirit. I didn't agree with them, but what could I do? I accepted my fate, my complete surrender to the geometric merging. I understood this chapter was finished and, in order to cross over successfully, I had to renounce my ego and identity. That was the moment when thought, emotion, and even my breathing, came to a halt.

Silence.

And then, a miracle happened. I don't know what caused it. Suddenly, I was consumed by a desire to return to humanity, as a human being. To live. Here. Not "there."

I started uttering phrases related to my life in the normal world. "Alon, I love you!" I shouted over and over, without knowing if he existed and could hear me. "Layla and Sahar, I love you!" I shouted to my niece and nephew. I shouted, "I want children! I want to be a mother too!"

The powerful voice in my vision kept repeating: "In the world you're in now, you can't be with people, you can't see nephews or partners, you can't have children. These things are no longer part of your life. Surrender yourself to the pleasure of unification with the other world, now you are part of the power of creation, stop wanting, kill the ego."

But I kept resisting. Without stopping, I went on: "I want children. Alon, I love you. Sahar and Layla, I love you. I want children now. Now. Alon, I love you." At the same time, I continued to feel physical pleasure, but it was forced, I didn't surrender myself to it. I stopped groaning, even though my body wanted to. I fought against the urge with all my might. I don't know how long my shouting continued.

In my opinion when Alon calls out "Kis, Kis, Kis".

I opened my eyes. Alon looked like a 3D character, very tall, and his features appeared as if they had come straight out of the Avatar movie. I still couldn't speak but I had finally managed to open my eyes. Alon helped me to my feet, even though I didn't believe standing was possible. I leaned on him and he slowly led me around the room.

"I want to get out of here, I have to get out of here," I pleaded. Alon hugged me. Later, I learned that his experience had been equally challenging. He was used to being the one who always wanted to leave, and was happy we were of one mind.

"I'm never going to get out of it, I'm never going to get out of it," I told him and myself over and over again. I shouted at Ayahuasca, "Get out of my body! I want you out of my body! I want to have children. I want to make them now. Where are Sahar and Layla? I won't get out of it, I won't get out of it. Leave my body now!" From the moment he woke me and I opened my eyes, I wouldn't stop talking to and biting myself.

At first he was still with me. "You *will* get out of it," he said and hugged me. But I was relentless, until he finally screamed, "Stop talking to yourself already! It's freaking me out!"

The last person who had issued such an order was my older sister Nilli, when I was five and speaking to my imaginary friends. At one point, I finally stopped.

We went outside. Alon told me that the ceremony had ended half an hour before I had woken up and Erin the shaman had tried to wake me. I couldn't remember Erin being present. Where was he? Didn't he notice that I was in distress?

We went back to the mattress, where I made good use of the yellow bucket. Alon held my forehead as I threw up. Yaniv, who reported having an amazing experience, was knocked out by the ceremony. His friend had a less intense one, but she was still under the influence of the trip and wanted to rest. We were supposed to sleep in the yurt that night, but I wasn't staying there another second.

We said as much to Erin.

"That's a shame," he muttered, and went on tidying up the space.

This is the shaman who was supposed to take care of us?

Alon took it upon himself to become the responsible adult in the group. He gathered all of us together, packed our belongings, downloaded the Uber app, and even communicated with the taxi driver in broken Portuguese. What an amazing man I have, I thought, I'm so lucky.

On the way back, I was a broken record: "Now. I want to have children with you now. Right away." All the insights became clear. My spiritual search was over. It wasn't that I had all the answers — I was just tired of the questions. I was done seeking advice from spiritual guides, done with distant dimensions and enlightenment. The amount of energy that my consciousness expended following these searches — to reach the "there" instead of "here," my idealization of the spiritual dimension, and the "mind loop" regarding where to go and what to be — had deprived me of being present through the most precious experience of all: being a human being in this place called Earth. I liked being here. I liked gravity. Thoughts. Emotions. Personal relationships. Connecting to my body. Even wanting money. I didn't want to surrender to something abstract and greater than myself.

Everything true was right here in front of me. Life. Our creation. I wanted to have children now. With the man in my life. In one sweeping moment, all the nonsense I had been carrying around in my consciousness was cast aside, and I was left with limitless gratitude for life.

In the taxi, we were mostly silent. Every few minutes I said: "I can't believe I did this to myself. I'm shocked by what just happened."

Back at Rosemary, Yaniv made us each a bowl of granola. The four of us snuggled up in bed and shared our experiences. Yaniv's had been amazing. He had learned about the secrets of creation and met beings of light. Alon confronted fears and demons, but managed to remain grounded. Yaniv's friend didn't allow herself to experience much of anything. After drinking the same substance and inhabiting the same room, we had encountered four vastly different worlds.

THE FOLLOWING DAY I REALIZED that I may have appeared the same as always on the outside, but I didn't recognize myself on the inside. I had new kinds of thoughts, and all the issues I was used to thinking about, such as how to advance, things to work on and what someone had said, were no longer present in my mind. What was present was expansiveness.

I still saw bright-colored geometric shapes every time I closed my eyes, but my dreams were vastly different. For example, I dreamt of a curly brunette who would stick her hands in my armpits and would not stop no matter how hard I screamed that it tickles. This is what I had felt with the Ayahuasca, that it was telling me: "I'm entering into your most sensitive and delicate places. It's hard, but you have to hold on. It will open up something inside you." I was less frightened and inhibited now, but still suffered from thought loops, and worried that they wouldn't go away.

I saw photos that Alon had taken of me outside the yurt, minutes before the ceremony began, and didn't recognize myself. Despite my colorful dress, I looked pale, and my expression seemed dazed and disoriented. I realized that I could have died there, and afterwards an online article would circulate about a stupid Israeli girl who went insane during an Ayahuasca ceremony, tagged with this strange photo.

I had flashbacks of the numerous times I proclaimed "I love you" and the crazy groaning. I recalled how I couldn't stand up, walk or open my eyes. I was stunned by how fragile and precious our existence is. That trip could have cost me my sanity, or even my life. Like so many others, I was vulnerable.

It turns out that, like so many others, I needed people around me, that we all needed each other. I didn't have to navigate the world alone. I had decided to come back from the abstract world for the people I loved.

At night I felt helpless every time I shut my eyes and saw the geometric images that the Ayahuasca had given rise to. I couldn't crave material things. I was scared that I would go crazy and that my brain would never be what it once was. I tried thinking about pre-ceremony things: my dream of giving a TED talk or setting up my international women's movement. But it didn't work. The thoughts wouldn't stabilize and I had a hard time falling asleep.

We were about to leave Brazil, and had a whole day of flights and driving ahead of us to reach the sex therapist workshop in Arizona.

ON THE WAY TO ARIZONA, MY BRAIN BECAME a place I felt more comfortable in. After Alon fell asleep on the flight, I connected to the plane's Wi-Fi and started reading business articles about Facebook and the infringement on users' privacy. It helped me fall asleep. I guess I just needed the mundane for a while, because when I tried listening to a recorded meditation, stressful images bombarded me. I understood that my consciousness was still very delicate.

After the Ayahuasca ceremony, I felt just how significant certain mistakes can be. My mistake with the Companion ticket seemed trivial in comparison, but the arrogance of this Y generation led me to believe that when I felt something intuitively, when it appeared in my vision, when the song that played in the background or person I met on the street all pointed to the same thing — it meant I should follow those signs.

I don't regret it, there is no point in regret, but I can say I acted without discretion, surrendering myself to the ceremony without holding my ground. I thought that even if Alon didn't want to come with me, I'd do the ceremony alone, and my greatest mistake was drinking those three glasses. I really don't know if my brain would have survived the experience in one piece if Alon hadn't been there to help me land. I have friends who can't sleep with the door shut to this day after a bad trip. It's no joke, the damage can be irreversible.

These things pointed to a place inside me that didn't respect the life I had here, my sanity, my health and my sensitivity. I managed my life as if it was a Netflix series, motivated by what would sell better and sound more adventurous. I didn't appreciate that I was human.

Alon trusted me and I had led us astray. I felt confusion, disorientation, and shame. From being the one who always knew the way, I became lost. Alon still looked at me without judgement and I melted into that. I had always thought that I was the leader in our relationship, and Alon the follower. But Alon already knew what his needs were without needing a workshop to tell him.

WE REACHED THE SEX THERAPIST COURSE. We weren't planning to be therapists, but saw it as the continuation of our sexuality studies. There were 40 participants, mostly American, and, unlike us, they were all there because they really wanted to practice sex therapy.

The workshop was intense. For ten days, from morning to night, we learned techniques, practiced them on each other, received feedback, and then practiced again. Unlike other workshops, where people had also come to play, people here came to work.

As always, the highlight was the people we met. I could speak openly and freely with them, about my miscarriage, my trauma from the Ayahuasca ceremony, the message I was trying to convey — the connection between sexuality and professional fulfillment in women. The most memorable conversation was with Albert, a married man who was polyamorous. He had one child and many partners.

Alon and I were monogamous. It's true that at the workshops we sometimes practiced with other people, but only within very clear boundaries and only at the workshops, with both of us typically present in the room.

Polyamorous people, on the other hand, have intimate relationships, with all that the word implies, with more than one person, including texts, presents, arguments, jealously, expectations, heart-to-heart talks and, of course, sex. I don't judge this lifestyle, but I find it hard to understand how people find the time for it. Alon and I barely managed to find enough time for each other. Albert explained that the key was a supportive community. And that his whole life revolved around the choice to be polyamorous.

We sat down for lunch together and he told me about his job as a salesperson in hi-tech.

"I want to find a way to share the power of what we're learning here with more people," I told him. I hoped that his ability to live both in the spiritual and business world would help me gain a better sense of what I wanted to do.

"Why do you want to make this knowledge accessible to others?" he asked.

"I think it will help people in other areas, for example, in their careers. It's really changed my life," I said.

"So, tell them to join us here, at the sexuality workshops," he replied and placed his hand on mine.

"Not everyone would want to participate in a workshop like this," I said and removed his hand. "A lot of people find what we do here bizarre. People who see themselves as mainstream."

"Why do you want to help "normal" people?" asked Albert. He explained that when he initially set out on this path, he wanted to receive the approval of those working with him.

"But those who discover the world of wizardry," he added with twinkling eyes, "no longer want to remain in the world of the normal."

"Isn't that a little condescending?" I asked. "You're implying that whoever seeks these kinds of experiences is superior to those who don't."

"I have no problem with normal people leading a normative life," he clarified. "I'm happy to meet someone who only wants to visit these worlds, to experience and experiment. But my condition is that we have to meet in the world of magic."

"Nicely put," I mumbled and went back to my quinoa.

I thought about this "world of magic." It sounded romantic, but that world had almost made me lose my sanity at the Ayahuasca ceremony a few days ago. Now more than ever, I needed to seek that which was accessible and grounded. I suddenly understood the women who were angry at us in Double You when we presented sexuality contents without sufficient preparation and mediation. Our job now was to make this information available to people in a way that would allow them to contain it. Maybe I could learn from Albert's experience with that.

I raised my head from my plate and said: "I'm trying to find a way to communicate a message about sexuality to women hearing about it for the first time."

"What do you do in your workshops for women?" he asked.

"We work on connecting them to their unique style of leadership."

"You mean female empowerment?"

"We try to avoid that expression. Women are not weak— we want to help them remember their unique strength, and understand that they are powerful by virtue of their being. The world urgently needs the wisdom and empathy that women possess. They can heal and improve the systems that run our lives."

"No argument there. But why do you think it's important that leaders learn about their sexuality?"

Albert's question broke the floodgates open: "Sexuality extends far beyond what happens in the bedroom," I said. "Until we cleanse the wound in our sexuality that festered from years of oppression, we will forever remain victims in all realms of society. When a woman is used to the idea that a man's needs and opinions take precedence, a world is created in which women don't know their own pleasure and strength. And so, we remain stuck in an vicious circle of dependency and pleasing. You mentioned women's empowerment? In my view there is nothing that empowers a woman more than knowing and giving priority to her own pleasure."

Albert started smiling and became more attentive.

I continued, "A woman's power is also related to her ability to experience pleasure, set boundaries, say yes or no, in the workplace, at home, in any space. Her sexuality, if given the right attention, connects her to extraordinary powers and allows her to realize that she is also important and deserving."

At this point I noticed that Albert was getting excited. With a glint in his eye, he leaned his hands against the table and moved closer to me.

"Women who don't think their pleasure is important in the bedroom," I continued, "won't believe that their opinion counts in the boardroom, and consequently won't end up pursuing their ideas outside the boardroom. Until we stop looking for a man to follow, we won't be able to connect to our strengths and follow *them* instead."

Albert suddenly closed up like a clam. He leaned back and turned his gaze to the side, staring into space.

"What are you thinking?"

"I was with you up until the 'stop looking for a man to follow'," he said. "What's the problem with following men? There are men who follow women too."

"I have no problem with men! On the contrary, I love men," I said enthusiastically. "Men have contributed, are contributing and will continue contributing to humanity. But you represent a particular side. And so many systems, among them the working world itself, is constructed in a way that answers only to your needs. It's not because you don't care about women, it's just what you know, because your perspective is limited. Now it's our turn to build a world that suits us *too*. Alongside men, not in place of them."

"So, what do you expect men to do in order to change the situation?" asked Albert.

"I expect men to go along with the change taking place in the world right now," I stressed. "We need more women leading and managing. The world is waiting for the solutions women have to offer in various fields: politics, education, business, balancing home and work... But too many talented women work for someone else instead of promoting their own ideas. We won't produce female leaders if we don't begin prioritizing our ideas and opinions. Many of the feminist movements to date are focused on demanding room to lead and equal rights. It's time for women to invite the men into a world which we are shaping. But the change is first and foremost internal — we have to connect to the voice inside of us and hear what it is saying."

"I can relate to many of the things you're saying, but I must say, it sounds like you have a problem with men. It sounds like you're angry with us, and I don't believe you can instill change with anger."

"It's true, there is anger in me," I admitted. This time I was the one who looked away. "I'm angry about all the energy I've wasted trying to get some man to understand me, trying to meet his approval, to hire me to work in his company so that I could be a part of something 'big.'

"I'm angry about the years I wasted as a young adult trying to please men in the bedroom, being thin enough for their taste, instead of exploring and discovering my sexuality and my body. It pains me to see so many women shortchanging themselves in their personal and professional lives, downgrading their dream to a hobby that they have no time for, because at the end of the day they are too tired from doing things that leave them empty.

"It might not seem like it at first glance, but I learned from my own experience and saw it in women I've had the privilege of working with — the belief that our ideas are important, and that the courage to prioritize ourselves and follow our authentic will are directly linked to sexuality, and sexuality is related to action, power, clarity, vision, creativity, a sense of female kinship, emergent skills and resources. They say that creating only-women forums drives the sexes apart and reinstates the status quo, but for many years our voice has been silenced and now we need a moment of quiet and time alone to hear it again."

"Sounds like you've got it," said Albert, but I could see that he wasn't with me, that I had antagonized him.

"I see that this is raising some objections in you," I called him out. "I want to bring forth something unifying, not alienating, but I'm not yet sure how. If you can see something that I can't, I'd appreciate it if you'd share it with me."

"OK, I'll be honest with you. I think you still have work to do regarding the way you perceive men. There's something there you still don't fully get. You might be repressing it. Try to use the space here in the workshop to reach a better understanding."

Maybe there was something to what he was saying. I noticed that even now, when a sensitive man whose feedback I had solicited, and who listened intently, made a comment, all I really wanted was for him to stop talking already and tell me I was right.

AT THE WORKSHOP WE WERE ASKED TO ASSUME THE ROLE OF THERAPISTS, to staunch people's sexual wounds and offer a helpful response. To work on my relationship with men, I tried to perform the exercises with male partners. One day it was with a tall French man named David who was in his forties. We were learning about pressure points in the body which release emotion.

During the exercise, I pressed on such points (near the armpit, two points on the chest and others) and invited him to breathe. He lay on the mat, his eyes closed, surrendering himself to the exercise with great vulnerability — shouting, crying, inhaling deeply. Tears came to my eyes. I was moved to witness him with his defenses down. I thought: how hard it is to be a man in the world these days. People expect you to be "strong," even if it means disregarding your emotions and needs.

That evening at the workshop we held a ceremony to heal the male and female aspects in each of us. Forty people sat in two circles, an inner one and an outer one. The only light in the room emanated from the candles in the middle of the circle. The outer circle held the female energy and the inner, the male. Both circles included both sexes. Each person looked into the eyes of someone in the other circle and, when a gong sounded, a person from the outer circle moved right, and so the pairs changed.

We were instructed to regard each other as the elevated essences we were, the sacred being that each of us represents as pure masculinity and pure femininity. When I looked at the men, I saw something in them I hadn't seen before. I noticed a vulnerability in their eyes, and what I perceived as a fear of women. I thought about the pressure they were under, about how masculinity today was still so rigid.

At this point, while reveling in the change brought about by shared eye contact, I marveled that here, in just a few hours, I was already engaged in a healing process in my relationship with men. But when called to mind men I didn't get along with, to see if their image now evoked a positive or at least different emotion, I saw that the anger remained. Men with their defenses lowered are a very different animal from men who resonate an alpha energy, who enter a room and claim it, who interrupt mid-sentence without explaining why; who behave as if they are on Earth to be served. The next day at the workshop, I had a direct experience with this kind of creature.

WE WERE TAUGHT THAT EACH PERSON HAS FOUR INTERNAL FORCES AT WORK: BODY, MIND, SPIRIT AND ANIMAL. They told us that to secure inner peace, we needed to make room for each of these elements within us, that because our mind compels our body to respond to its needs, the visceral force is given almost no room. At first, I had no idea what they were talking about. What did they mean by "the animal"?

We practiced all kinds of exercises that illustrated this concept. In one, we were separated into couples, one portraying a predator and the other his prey. Alon chose to be a wolf and I, a rabbit. While wolf Alon was on the prowl, I was hopping around innocently, munching on grass. That feeling of not knowing when the wolf would rear his head was both scary and thrilling.

When Alon attacked me, I tried to fight for my life, but the hierarchy in the animal kingdom forced me to surrender, and I accepted my inevitable end. It was a powerful experience to give in like that. I lay on a blue mattress and Alon leaned over me, growling and even nipping at my neck. His large paws pinned my shoulders to the mattress.

Around us were about twenty other couples performing the same exercise; every few seconds we heard someone else being hunted down and variations of beastly growls. I breathed heavily and kept my eyes shut. I couldn't deny that I had felt pleasure in being dominated by a powerful predator.

And of course, there is also pleasure in dominating. When I was the predator, the same tension as before came into play. This time I was a lion and Alon a squirrel. I waited for the right moment, then charged at him while growling from deep inside my throat: "You're mine."

Another exercise involved making out while the facilitator instructed us when to act from a spiritual place — gently, emotionally, attentively, and when from the inner animal — strong, aggressive, taking what you want.

That sexual advances moved between gentle and visceral, allowing us to feel the pleasure in each of the forms. I was straddling Alon, our legs spread and our genitals touching under our clothes. When we were in animal mode, we kissed and moved forcefully, pulling each other's hair and groaning, and when our spiritual side kicked in we slowed down, gave each other gentle kisses on the neck, stroked each other's heads and whispered loving words into each other's ears. The moment the facilitator activated the beast again, the whisper transformed into aggressive licking that turned into biting, and so on and so forth. Usually Alon is gentle in the bedroom, but here he was full on beast. His character wanted to conquer, and my whole body wanted to surrender, which I hadn't anticipated. Surprisingly, that beast turned me on.

CHAPTER 6
MEETING THE ANIMAL

"The doors to the world of the wild self are few but precious. If you have a deep scar, that is a door, if you have an old, old story, that is a door. If you love the sky and the water so much you almost cannot bear it, that is a door. If you yearn for a deeper life, a full life, a sane life, that is a door."

Clarissa Pinkola Estés

ON THE LAST DAY OF THE THERAPIST WORKSHOP, we were taught how to identify what aroused us. They explained that as sex therapists, it was important to know how to manage our sexual energy instead of letting it manage us. For example, if a particular situation with a patient is liable to turn us on, we should rechannel the energy to avoid crossing ethical boundaries.

Many arousal triggers, they explained, are rooted in childhood. We learned about the theory of Jack Morin, an American psychologist who interviewed thousands of people and found four recurring categories:

1. Some people get turned on by people whose distance creates a sense of expectation and longing. For example, a long-distance or virtual relationship.

2. Some people become aroused by physical contact that breaks rules or taboos. For example, talking dirty, having sex with, or thinking sexually about, someone you shouldn't be, or having sex where you're not supposed to.
3. Some people are aroused by people with whom they are in a power dynamic — dominator and dominated, people who have social authority over them, etc.
4. Some people are turned on by ambivalence: being aroused by people they hate and love, are attracted to and disgusted by at the same time, and so on.

I knew without a doubt that I belonged to the third category. My fantasies were about people with whom I shared power dynamics. Before I started studying sexuality, one of my regular fantasies was total surrender to a powerful man. We meet at an event. He hears me speaking passionately about the social initiative I'm working on and desires me. He flatters, seduces and, after a few encounters, I'm his. At one point, I have to start asking for his approval for anything that I do. He doesn't rape me or force me into anything. In my fantasy we are playing a game. We both know that I can stop at any time, but I don't. What arouses him is feeling that I am under his absolute control, and what arouses me is that he's addicted to me.

When I shared this with some of my girlfriends, I discovered that many shared a similar fantasy — an aggressive man who subordinated them with their consent, something like *Fifty Shades of Grey*, BDSM style. But in my case, there was one notable difference – my fantasies were not only about men — they were also, maybe even mostly, about women. And they were always fat. Very fat.

THE FIRST TIME I REMEMBER MASTURBATING I was three. I would lie on my belly on the sofa, touch my genitals over my clothes with both hands and move my body up and down over and over again. I didn't really understand what I was doing, but at one point I understood it was not something you were supposed to do in public. It should be kept strictly private.

Only in the 7th grade, I discussed it with my friends for the first time. After they admitted that they masturbated with the showerhead, I showed them how I did it. They giggled in delight.

"I was sure something was wrong with me," I told them, and the giggles resumed.

As I grew up, I started fantasizing while doing it. In my fantasies I surrendered myself to large people, mostly women. At one point, because of those fantasies, I thought I might be a lesbian. In high school I experimented with friends. We all had boyfriends, but sometimes we would touch each other and laugh. It didn't really do anything for me, but it was funny and exciting because it was taboo.

Once I attended a lesbian event to explore the question more seriously. I was asked to wear a bracelet signifying that I was single, and I noticed someone who wouldn't stop looking at me, but when I had my chance, I wasn't interested. It just didn't turn me on.

In the past, I would ask my partners to imitate what I was doing when masturbating and touch me in a certain way over my clothes while I fantasized. I couldn't enjoy myself sexually without those thoughts. But when I started studying sexuality and becoming aware of my body, a strange thing happened: pleasure ceased during my fantasies about the aggressive character who subordinates me to his will. On the contrary, they brought pain to my Yoni. Perhaps, as a force of habit, I continued to feel turned on, but after a few minutes it would fade, and even become unpleasant, as if the Yoni knew it wasn't what she really wanted. At one point, I put these fantasies to rest and they stopped being part of my sexuality.

The facilitator at the workshop explained that what turns us on is often related to a childhood wound or deprivation. One of the participants shared that he was a younger brother to two older sisters who used to tease and hit him as a child, and to this day one of the things that aroused him was aggressive and violent behavior by women in bed.

"Now you'll get the opportunity to explore it," said the facilitator. "All of you will physically recreate one of your fantasies with the other participants. Be attentive to what is happening in your body. You can learn things from it that you might have not noticed before."

Instructed to split into groups of three, I scanned the room for Debbie. She was a large 50-year-old American woman, who appeared very comfortable in her body. She agreed to do the exercise together, and John, an Italian man in his 20s, fit, with black hair and brown eyes, joined us. I was the last one in the round.

While recreating the fantasy, we pretended that Debbie and I were in bed together with her taking the lead: she told me what to do and demanded that I stroke her hair, sing songs to her in a certain way; and she asked questions, abruptly changing the topics. I didn't give John a role, so he just supported us.

Nothing. Not only did I feel no attraction for Debbie — the entire exercise felt silly. Around us we heard groaning from other groups, which sounded artificial to me. I was uncomfortable and waited for the exercise to end.

But at one point something happened. While Debbie whispered in my ear how beautiful I was, she moved into a seated position and pulled me onto her lap. I didn't know why, but I felt fear creeping through my body, as if I was in danger. I had to get up, but she wouldn't let me at first, and then the whole situation started to close in on me. I froze. I felt my body melting into hers and images from my childhood came pouring into my head.

WHEN I WAS FOUR, we had a nanny named Miriam. She was an older, large woman with brown hair. She used to sit on an armchair in the hallway and place me on her lap by force. That was her way of quieting me when she thought I needed to calm down. When I tried to stand up, she wouldn't let me, and no matter how angry I got, how I shouted or squirmed, my fate was to remain on her lap. At one point, I would stop resisting. I don't think she was being intentionally abusive, she just wanted me to sit still, or maybe this was her way of getting some rest. (There's something pleasant about having a child on your lap while you're resting.) Either way, she imposed her will on me for extended periods.

I remembered myself sitting on her lap while my sisters watched TV or went to the bathroom, free to do as they pleased with their bodies. I also remembered the expression on her face when I would make a mess or go wild, just before she sat me down. She didn't look me in the eye, just stared at a distant point in the room, too tired to contain the energies of a toddler.

The images flooded my brain until the facilitators announced that the exercise was over. The other groups stopped what they were doing and sat in an open circle, but I was frozen, tears rolling down my cheeks. Suddenly, I felt a hand on my shoulder. It was John.

"Is everything OK?" he asked in a whisper. I nodded. Then another hand, this time Debbie's. I turned to her, and she looked for my smile, but couldn't find it.

The facilitator asked if anyone wanted to share. What had just happened? I recalled the process with Sanand, who commented that my body freezing up the way it did suggested I might have undergone some form of abuse. I thought about the years of stagnant sexuality. How could I enjoy myself and flow when what my default position was to surrender and freeze? I thought about the last two years in which I had avoided this fantasy because of the pain it caused my Yoni. I couldn't share it with the group. Instead, I went over to one of the facilitators during the break.

SAMUEL, A FACILITATOR FROM ITALY IN HIS FORTIES, had treated hundreds of people in Israel and around the world. I felt comfortable with him. For him there was no such thing as too perverted or weird. I told him about the fantasy I was exploring and what I was feeling.

"There are a few ways to explain what you're telling me," said Samuel. "You can take the path of traditional psychology, which means trying to understand your past and derive from it why that specific behavior with the nanny shaped your arousal patterns."

"What does that mean?" I asked.

"Our early experiences shape our personality in general and our sexuality in particular. For a child, the passion for life is a general passion," he said. "You just go with what feels good. Later, at a certain age, shame enters into the equation, because there are some things you can't do in public, or at all. As a result, the child suppresses passions and desires, some of which are sexual in nature. When we get older, our sexuality awakens, but now we are instructed to direct it to a specific person. This is part of our developmental process."

"I don't understand — you're saying that because of what happened with my nanny when I was a child, this kind of behavior turns me on?"

"According to your story, the nanny imposed something on you against your will until you gave in. As part of this surrender you experienced calmness. In masturbation you tried to recreate this. Perhaps because it was created as the result of a process you did not experience as positive, the more you become sexually connected to your body, the more your body reacts with pain, rather than pleasure."

Something about his explanation didn't put my mind at ease, it felt too superficial.

Samuel continued, "Look, this is only the psychological approach, which I respect but it happened thirty years ago, and we don't really have the ability to understand what actually happened. You could also approach it from a different direction."

"Which is?"

"You said that when you fantasized about it, it hurt and you stopped. But I understand that it still arouses you, right?"

"Yes... a little... I don't know. There's also the question of habits here."

"Habit or no habit — if it arouses you, it still exists in you. It sounds as if you have some more shadow work to do here."

"What's shadow work?"

"Shadow work is accessing hidden parts in ourselves. These repressed parts usually erupt from our subconscious to find forms of expression: existing in your fantasies while being unaware of your story."

"OK."

"I think that your fantasy isn't necessarily related only to the childhood incident. We all have a will to surrender ourselves and release control. In your case, it sounds like a real longing to surrender to something bigger than you."

"What do you mean? I don't have a longing to be raped by a man or a woman."

"Of course not. No one actually wants to be raped, but many fantasize about power dynamics in order to surrender themselves. The pain you feel when masturbating to what you described might not be because you want that, but your arousal can certainly derive from a deep will to surrender out of strength."

"I'm not sure I understand. How can I surrender out of strength?"

"Do you have an example of a situation in which you experienced complete surrender without calling up that fantasy? Something that contained such profound pleasure that you completely lost yourself in it?"

The answer scared me so much that I didn't say anything at first. "Ayahuasca," I finally replied.

"What happened in your Ayahuasca session?"

"It's hard to describe. I asked her to teach me what it's like to be her, and then in the trip I became an animal, and the animal went through my body and moved me, and I couldn't stop groaning… It sounds strange, I know, but it was a pleasure I'd never experienced before. It was terrifying, I almost lost my mind."

"There is no strange," he assured me. "It's the subconscious. If it scares you, it means you're on the right path. There's something about that animal inside you. Agree to meet her. Therein lies a key."

"How can I meet the animal? I'm never doing Ayahuasca again."

"You don't have to do Ayahuasca to meet her. Ask your subconscious to show you the way. Try reaching it by pleasuring yourself, in dreams, dancing, before falling asleep. If she appeared in your subconscious, then she's inside you. If you ask, she will come."

"Interesting."

"Very interesting. If you befriend your shadow, you'll find a lot of strength there. It's like a person learning to ride their dragon. You can also find healing for the harm you experienced and for your relationships."

I couldn't handle the exercises on the last day of the workshop — it was information overload. I had a lot of homework ahead of me: to work on my childhood trauma, to contain the whole concept of the shadow, to understand how it all related to my ambivalence towards men. It was too much for one week.

My Yoni had become my friend over time, and now it was telling me that it had had enough. I wouldn't practice with anyone except Alon and even with him it was hard. I took offense every time he paid attention to other women, and asked him to stop practicing with other people at the workshop. I felt as if it was scattering our energy and there was no justification for it anymore. Our sexuality had a good flow and what I wanted more than anything was to harness that energy and bring a child into the world.

A MONTH AFTER WE GOT BACK TO ISRAEL, WE WENT TO THE MIDBURN FESTIVAL, the Israeli version of Burning Man. Alon and I slept in a camp with friends and offered beginner sexuality workshops under a large red-colored dome. It was the first time we had facilitated this content and shared it with the world.

Our beginner workshop introduced basic principles of learning sexuality and allowed people to explore their inner animal. In addition, Tal Shavit, a friend and partner at *Double You*, and I, gave a women's-only workshop. Each of the workshops was fully booked. It was interesting to connect these different worlds, offering this content to friends; Even Alon's sister had signed up. I saw people intrigued, opening up, and experiencing.

Following one of the workshops, a woman walked up and introduced herself as Crystal. She was an American with braided light brown hair. She was wearing the typical Midburn outfit: a bra with sequins, a long skirt and a black pouch. She was good-looking, open and easy-going, but to my surprise, as she talked to me I realized she was actually shy.

Crystal spoke with a trembling voice: "You said at the start of the workshop that it used to be hard for you to reach an orgasm. I've never had an orgasm. Penetration hurts and I don't know how to approach it." A tear glistened in her eye. I knew her desperation well, that sinking feeling that it would never change. I listened to her but didn't know what to say. I asked for support from within: What should I tell her? How can I help her? I immediately had an image of myself ten years earlier, when I stopped taking the pill and didn't get my period for a year. After trying everything medicine had to offer, I went to a homeopath who looked into my eyes and said: "You'll get your period again. I'm sure of it."

I took her hand, looked into her eyes and said: "You will come, I'm sure of it." We both smiled. I could see she was expecting me to offer practical advice, but what did I really know? I shared tools I had acquired at the workshops to help her connect with her Yoni. "Even more than to a person," I explained, "learning how to come is connected to our relationship with our sexual organ". We talked about how she can try to befriend her Yoni, about how important pleasuring oneself is, going far beyond satisfying a need. It enables a dialogue with our Yoni and even helps connect to deep inner desires.

After the conversation, I went to my tent and took my own advice. I lay on the bed, made contact with my Yoni and got started. While doing so I thought about Samuel's words: "Agree to meet the animal. Call her and she will come." I didn't understand what I was doing, but I asked the abstract entity in my subconscious to reveal itself.

"Show me what to think about, how to turn this act into something illuminating."

At first, nothing. At one point dream fragments started appearing in my mind, but none of them was of a sexual nature. I imagined myself participating in women's circles across the globe, gathering the courage and, along with other women, expressing the message of female leadership and connection to the body through the written and spoken word.

The clearer the dreams were, the deeper the pleasure became. It took me a long time to reach an orgasm, but when I did, instead of a sense of release I felt vitality: I was filled with energy and a sense of competence. I later learned that there was a whole field of sexuality that focused on what I had just done. It's called Sex Magic.

SEX MAGIC IS THE PRACTICE OF USING AN ORGASM TO FULFIL INTENTIONS AND DREAMS.
I came across this term at a sexuality festival in the Israeli desert. An American named Laurie was the facilitator. Laurie was a colorful character in her 70s, with cropped blonde hair, full lips like mine, and a constant smile on her face. She was thin and short, with a sharp tongue and a sense of humor.

After sharing her life story and how she ended up in the field, she instructed each participant to write down a specific intention they hoped to fulfill.

"Be specific, not general," she said. "Write something that you can refer back to afterwards, if your intention is realized. But don't limit the universe — let it lead you in various ways."

I wrote that I wanted to become the mother of a healthy, happy child. Then Laurie instructed us to prepare the space. She said that the more seriously we took it, the stronger it would be.

"Imagine that you're in a temple," she said. "Bring flowers, incense, fresh sheets, make it romantic — something that, if your partner had designed it for you, would make you wet right away," she said and winked.

Then we did some emotional release exercises: shouting into a pillow, dancing and kicking our legs in the air, cleansing and releasing all the emotions that were stuck inside us and irrelevant to what we wanted to fulfill.

Then came the moment to declare the intention, to be phrased as if it were already a fact. In my case: "I'm the mother of a healthy, happy child."

And then we got down to business. If you were working alone, you had to start pleasuring yourself, building towards orgasm and then, approaching climax, to visualize the intent or request and utter it over and over again.

"Imagine you're shooting it into the galaxy," she said. "After you're done, breathe for three minutes and release it."

She explained that when performed as a couple, the exercise offered a surprising twist. If it was a man and woman, the man would dedicate himself to making the woman orgasm and serve her in this process. At this, many inquisitive hands shot up, but Laurie wasn't taking any questions or comments. She looked at us, laughed and said, "Wait, I'll explain it." You could see how much she liked talking about this subject.

She believed that a woman's orgasmic potential was linked to the human potential of love on Earth.

"One of the problems women have is that they can't completely connect to their femininity because they won't surrender themselves to the man in front of them. In this exercise, men can support a woman's process of surrendering."

There were still hands raised in the air. Laurie fielded a question.

"So, what happens after she comes? What about the man's intentions?"

"Excellent," said Laurie. "The man concentrates on the woman coming. He offers himself as the one to serve her in the process. When the woman comes, she dedicates her orgasm to both their intentions. Her orgasm connects to all the orgasms women have had since time immemorial and sends both their visions into the cosmos. It also aids in undoing the suppression women have suffered since time immemorial. In this way the man pays respect to the woman without asking for anything in return. Her orgasm takes center stage and the magic they create together."

Wow, I thought to myself.

"OK, here we go," said Lorrie and turned the lights off. "I suggest giving the women a breast massage, because it releases oxytocin and jumpstarts the process. Good luck!"

All the participants lay on mattresses, shut their eyes and covered themselves with a blanket. While practicing on myself, the sentence played over and over again in my head: "I'm the mother of a healthy, happy child."

TWO WEEKS LATER I WAS OVULATING. In the afternoon we started touching, which evolved into Alon giving me a Yoni massage. I released a lot of pain. That night we had sex. It was nice but also painful, probably from pent-up emotion that the earlier massage hadn't released. I asked Alon to pull out. In a situation like this, he usually would, but this time something different happened: a life impulse surged inside Alon. He didn't want to pull out. He stopped moving and looked into my eyes like the animal that loved me most in the world. It completely opened me up and the pain vanished. Looking back at him, I said to myself: that's it. This is my man. Those brown eyes, his sexual urge, the kindness and love he has for me. It was a real moment. As real as it gets.

I felt at one with life and marveled by how delicate it all was. We live only once and all we have is the now, so we had better live well, and feel as much as possible. I gave thanks for reaching this stage, for finding the courage to try to bring a child into the world with the man I loved. A grown man. A grown man who was still young.

I bought several pregnancy tests after that night. I checked each day until I had received five consecutive negative results. I sensed that I was pregnant and couldn't understand why the tests didn't concur. "I'm getting only one line, but I think I'm pregnant," I told my mom.

"Let me check it tonight and I'll get back to you tomorrow," she replied. My mother has this ceremony in which she asks a question at bedtime and in the morning wakes up with the answer. I don't know if the answers come from her subconscious or her heart or from some divine guidance. The important thing is that she's right.

The next day she texted me on WhatsApp: "You're pregnant with a boy."

I believed her. I believed my body. I stopped checking.

WE WENT TO THE DESERT FOR A FRIENDS' WEDDING. I was so happy they were getting married that I let myself indulge in two glasses of wine. In a few hours we were flying to a leadership convention in Berlin the next day, where I was going to lecture on the connection between female leadership and the body for the first time. Taking advantage of every minute, I danced wildly for a good stretch of the celebration. At one point, I suddenly felt something tear inside me. Pain shot through me. I ran to find Alon, then lay down in the corner of the *zula* relaxing area.

"What's the matter?" Alon asked in alarm.

"Something's happening to my body," I said. "Maybe it's left over from the miscarriage? Maybe my appendix? Not good."

Alon stroked me. We rested until it was time to go to the airport.

We landed in Berlin and went to our hotel. While Alon went out to meet some friends who had also come for the convention, the pain persisted. I called Alon and said: "Buy more pregnancy tests — I've got to understand what's happening."

Half an hour later Alon was back.

"I bought two kinds to be on the safe side," he said handing me the tests. The first came out positive. So did the second. We couldn't take the smiles off our faces.

The next day I gave my lecture. Even though I was well-prepared, I went onto the stage full of fear, even shaking a little. I was scared by the fact that facilitators from sexuality workshops I had attended were in the audience, and even more intimidated by all the regular people who had come to hear standard material on the topic of leadership. I was afraid of being misunderstood, making mistakes, and I also had this primordial, irrational fear that if I talked about sexuality in public, I would be burned at the stake.

I told myself that no matter what, this is what I have to offer. Guided by the sensations in my womb, I shared the following:

"I remember the day I had my first real orgasm. I was 26 years old. In my bed. In the afternoon. The ceiling was spinning and I suddenly burst out into uncontrollable laughter. I experienced sensations I never had before. My partner asked: 'Why are you covering your face?' I didn't even realize I was. I was hiding. I was embarrassed. 'Move your hands from your face. Stretch them out. Celebrate your pleasure,' he said, and for the first time, that's what I did. I said yes to my sexuality.

"In my lecture today I will talk about the importance of 'yes' and 'no', and about how our approach to our sexuality as women increases our power in our personal and professional relationships. I will share what I have learned in the past few years working with more than 1,000 women from 14 different countries, among them entrepreneurs just starting out, executives in large hi-tech firms, successful businesswomen and women in lower socio-economic realities.

"But most of all, I will share my long personal journey which led me to experience positive sexuality. At 10, when I went over to a friend's house, a stranger on the street flashed his penis at me and I ran as fast as I could. At 15 I took my first summer job, selling ice cream on the beach. My boss, who was 45 at the time, used to squeeze my behind with both hands every time I walked by, and I would move away with a polite smile. At 20, working in sales, my first time for a startup, a client placed his hand on my thigh in the middle of a meeting.

"Many people, mostly men, who hear these stories, will wonder if I provoked it. They can't imagine what it's like to go through life as a woman. Shifting the blame to me made me wonder whether I was sending out sexual energy. I realized that in order to be safe, I had to stop.

"My first orgasm was the first time I could contain and accept my own sexuality. The pleasure was so profound that I walked around for hours with a sense of confidence and power entrenched deep inside my body. I couldn't stop smiling. I remember standing in line at the grocery store, realizing that my incessant smiling probably looked weird. People I had met that day said: 'You're radiant. You look marvelous.' That feeling stayed with me for more than 24 hours. At work, I was exceptionally productive. It was the best version of me that I knew.

"Like many women, I never received tools to approach my sexuality directly. I remember thinking, if sexuality has so much value in our lives, why is no one teaching us how to use it?

"After experiencing the power that orgasm has over life, I decided to expand my knowledge on the subject. I first turned to my good friend Google and searched 'how to be a sexual person,' 'how to approach our sexuality,' and 'how not to freeze in sexual situations.' To my surprise, the results that I found most useful were on websites that discussed workshops for learning about sexuality and tantra.

"When I told my friends I was going to attend a sexuality workshop, their reactions were, 'Wow, have fun. It's called tantra, right? I know what it is, I've seen videos of the positions they teach online.' But far from being focused on positions, our workshop explored emotional relationships, boundaries and the ability to communicate yes and no authentically, in every area of life.

"From the workshop I learned three transformative principles. The first is the importance of saying 'no,' which extends far beyond the bedroom. It means saying 'no' to anything that doesn't serve us in life. Our teacher taught, "A person who has no 'no' is a person who has no 'yes.'" We can't recognize our 'yes' when we're constantly compromising. If we don't let go of the things we don't want, we won't have time for the things we do.

"In the past, when I led an initiative with partners, most of my challenges involved board meetings. During those meetings I was relatively quiet, because I was considered the least experienced person in the room. In addition, because I was the only woman, I was afraid of saying the wrong thing. After the workshop I decided to start practicing my 'no' there, of all places, where it was the hardest. Afraid at first, I started by saying 'no' to someone who called a remark I made 'irrelevant.' It felt so good I turned it into a habit.

"'No, I don't think we should pursue this project, it isn't good for us.' 'No, I won't invite that person for an interview just to be polite, because I know we will not recruit him.' And so on. After I started, I couldn't understand why I hadn't started sooner. My partners respected my 'no' and realized that 'no' means no.

"Gradually, as my confidence increased, I could start working on 'yes.' After we finally define our 'no,' the next stage is to understand our 'yes.' This is the second principle I learned at the sexuality workshop. It's called our 'hell yes' — our absolute or total yes. There is a saying that we practice: 'If it's not a 'hell yes' then it's a 'no,' which is a little reminiscent of the saying 'If there's any doubt, there is no doubt.'

"We were taught that in order to reach any decision you have to have a yes on three different levels: mind (rational), heart (emotional) and body (physical). You have to ask the mind, 'what do you think should be done?', ask the heart, 'what do you feel should be done?', and consult with the body about the different options. From the moment this idea was introduced to me, I learned to listen to my body, and most of the background noise during the decision-making completely disappeared.

"For me, discovering my 'hell yes' was discovering my authority. I started trusting my decisions. From that moment on, I didn't have to seek my partners' approval and rely on them to make decisions for me. Furthermore, I developed higher standards regarding things that I would say yes to. I used to spend hours sitting at meetings that didn't interest me, the kind I knew didn't have any real value for anyone in the room. Since then, I just stopped.

"The third principle was the most important one of all. It was the one that allowed me to internalize my 'yes' and 'no' on another level, and that was learning to understand and communicate my boundaries.

"There is one exercise I remember especially well. I stood at one side of the room and my partner on the other. After each step, I instructed my partner to take one step back, forward, or to stay where he was. This seemingly virtual exercise was very significant to me.

"I'd heard plenty over the years about inappropriate sexual conduct, but this was the first time I experienced appropriate sexual conduct. It felt like I had received a fountain of essential knowledge, a hidden treasure, which allowed me as a female human being to walk the world with strength and power.

"To my great surprise, the place where I felt it most acutely was at work. We have no idea the extent to which the way we deal with our sexuality influences our ability to take up space, how it can shrink us in our professional relationships, how much power there is to be derived from owning our sexuality, our energy, our presence.

"Prior to the process I had undergone, when someone stood so close I could smell his breath, I would make myself concentrate on what he had to say while praying for the nightmare to end. After the workshop, when I found myself in a situation like this, I'd just say: 'Excuse me, could you please take a step back?' In the past, if someone placed his hand on my leg at a meeting, I would freeze or at best politely push it away. After the workshop, when I knew my boundaries, it became: 'Why are you touching my leg? Move your hand away please.'

"The more 'sexually educated' I became, able to discern the delicate energy of sexuality and the subconscious places that harm us and others, the easier it became to understand the paralyzing factors or the placating that arises in response. At the same time, I learned about the positive place that provides us with energy and fills us with creativity and passion. I couldn't understand why we weren't learning this at school, much less in the workplace.

"It's no wonder many of us freeze, many of us are embarrassed, live in fear, don't know how to identify our boundaries and certainly not how to communicate and protect them. We were not educated about the strongest energy that drives our life.

"I want to do something about that. I want to encourage more women to explore their 'yes' and their 'no,' their boundaries, in a way that will affect their personal and professional relationships. It's not easy for me to stand on this stage and raise this flag, but I've decided to defend this passion because I know that now is our time as women to lead the way. And it starts with the basics of learning our 'yes' and our 'no.'

"In one of our workshops, we assigned an exercise that allowed women to come into contact with their no. They had to walk around the room, meet each other and ask for something random. The rule was that no matter what someone asked for, you had to say no. The requests could be trivial, such as: 'Can we meet tomorrow?' or 'Can you help me prepare this presentation?' The response had to be no,' to see how it felt.

"Jess, a 36-year-old German woman, burst into tears in the middle of the exercise. She told me: 'I realized I never knew how to say 'no' and now I understand the professional and personal price I've paid for it.' But it's not only the 'no' we have a hard time with. It's also the 'yes.' One of the things that surprised me the most was how speechless we were when asked a simple question: 'What do you want?'

"In one of our workshops for teenage girls I met Eliza, a 17-year-old who was cleaning homes to financially support her parents. Eliza was talented and bright. At one of our workshops she said: 'No one has ever asked me to say out loud what I want.' Later in the workshop she felt confident enough to share: 'What I really want is to become a school principal.'

"We are finally living in a time when women can speak loudly about what we don't allow people to do with our body, our rights, our wages. We are clearly saying — no. No more. But saying no and taking responsibility for our boundaries is only the first step to realizing our potential and power as women. We also have to comprehend and communicate what we *do* want: life can and should bring us pleasure and fulfillment. We're not only here to survive, we're here to flourish, to know pleasure in our private lives, to take a leading role in guiding men how to behave with a woman's body and our needs, to follow our curiosity and realize our ideas. And so, while supporting women around the world who are currently being sexually exploited, we are also creating a world in which we are no longer the victims, a world in which we lead.

"I've noticed that when women start implementing 'yes' and 'no' in their personal lives they also start doing it in their professional lives. They demand to be given equal wages, take part in decision making, and create work environments that correspond to their needs and to lead the public discourse. And men, this is also relevant to your daughters, your sisters, your partners.

"So what can you do? First, men and women at the management level — it's time to give your employees, of both genders, tools to communicate their 'yes' and their 'no.' When you bring new employees into your workplace and train them, consider incorporating exercises that teach sexual behavior — teaching employees to set their boundaries and develop a healthy dialogue on the subject.

"Women, now that we're experiencing this revolution, finally saying what we are no longer willing to withstand, let's make sure we don't forget our 'yes.' Let's explore it, invest in it, demand it in various aspects: our body, our money, our ideas, our life. Together we are building a world in which our 'no' is clearly heard and our 'yes' is accepted. A world in which we make ourselves available for our own pleasure and strength is a better world for everyone."

My baby was an embryo when I communicated this message for the first time. I thought what a great start this was to my pregnancy and that I would continue developing and sharing this message throughout it.

But my body had other plans.

BEFORE I GOT PREGNANT, I IMAGINED THAT DURING THE PREGNANCY I WOULD BE HAPPY AND VITAL, but for the first few months I actually felt very weak. I felt on the verge of fainting, threw up a lot and my mood was low. I would almost define it as despair, as if nothing could save me. There was no external source of energy from which I could draw strength.

At work and during meetings I was distracted so it was easier, but getting through the rest of the day was an ordeal. I tried every technique: I luxuriated in longs baths, sang in the living room, improvised voices, danced to Beyoncé on full volume, dabbled in writing exercises, worked out and even did some drawing. I practiced guided imagination in preparation for the birth, tried Osho's emotional release exercises, read moving texts and cried a lot. All that helped, but only temporarily.

Despair became my natural state during those weeks, and for no good reason. I was simply sad. For the first time I understood people who have a hard time getting out of bed or who take pills.

Bedtime was the roughest. I suddenly withdrew from Alon. It was strange to be pregnant and feel isolated. I wanted him to touch me and show me love constantly, but no matter how much warmth he gave, I still felt alone.

During that time, I made a date with my sisters to celebrate our mother's birthday. We have a family tradition of going around the room and sharing how we feel.

"I feel awful," I burst into tears when it was my turn. "I'm sad all the time. I don't understand what's wrong with me. I can't find any meaning in anything. I'm bored. I don't feel like doing anything. It's hard to get out of bed in the morning. To function. It's been like this for weeks and it's not going away." This was the first time I had admitted this to anyone except Alon.

The three of them looked at me. Natalie and Nilli hugged me. My mother, seated across from me, leaned forward and quoted, "'If you're going through hell — keep going.' Don't be afraid of the dark. You're going through hormonal changes and you need to be sensitive to them. It will be OK. Make sure you get out of the house often enough and in the meantime, don't let yourself drown."

When I started reading about it, I realized I had perinatal depression. There is a low percentage of women (some sources claim around 20%) who experience depression at the start of their pregnancy. It seemed I was sensitive to the hormonal changes and would have to be careful even after giving birth. I didn't want to go to a doctor for an official diagnosis. I was worried that they would try to persuade me to take pills. I decided to try and cope myself, and it was tough.

I cancelled all my scheduled business trips, including one of the most important global financial forums in China, which I was looking forward to, and kept only one non work-related one.

A few months before the pregnancy we had signed up to be assistants in the beginners' sexuality workshop, where we had begun our journey. Being assistants meant, that in addition to participating in the workshop like everyone else, we would lead a pod, a smaller sharing circle, in which we would listen and offer support.

I wasn't sure how appropriate it would be to go to a sexuality workshop while pregnant, but who knew when we would be able to attend another one after becoming parents?

WE ARRIVED IN ITALY AND DROVE TO A PLACE THAT WAS AN HOUR AND A HALF FROM ROME. Forty people came to the workshop, set in a center surrounded by green hills. Apart from us and the kitchen staff, which surprisingly included two Israelis, everyone was European.

One of the facilitators at the workshop was Lea, an uninhibited woman with a unique facilitating style. Keeping her words to a minimum, she sometimes stopped before everyone had understood her instructions and then communicated the rest with her body.

This time, she was facilitating the self-pleasure ceremony, the same ceremony that had caused Alon to almost up and run during our first workshop together. I lay on a mattress in the corner of the mostly-darkened room and kept my eyes open. The facilitators stood nearby. The instructions were very short and allowed ample time for everyone to touch themselves beneath the blanket. In the background, tribal music was playing and Lea moving and dancing ecstatically. As I closed my eyes, my body started acting of its own accord.

Instead of pleasuring myself the usual way, I danced while lying down, gliding my hands from side to side, moving my mouth, making noises, gently biting my hands. It felt so good. It was as if the animal I had wanted to make contact with had come to visit and was expanding my consciousness. I sensed my womb, more deeply with every song that played, until I could actually feel the fetus inside my body.

I started to sing to him and he started to sing through me. "Mommy, I'm not afraid," he sang. "I'm coming to Earth and I'm not afraid. I'm happy to come here." Tears of joy rolled down my cheeks. For an hour I was in a session of inner communication and movement.

Immediately afterwards, I took my clothes off and walked around the hall. I went outside and strolled along the grass. I wanted to draw powers from the soil beneath my feet. My heart was open. I was prepared for motherhood. I was here on Earth, in all its totality, thankful to God for being born a woman.

WHEN I WENT BACK INSIDE I SAW ALON DANCING BY THE CANDLES IN THE MIDDLE OF THE ROOM, celebrating life. It was hard to believe that this was the ceremony that had almost made him drop out of the workshop. In the past, we had come as two people searching for something to connect us and now we were one unit. Wedded to each other through these processes.

We also did a Yoni massage at the workshop. At this point, Alon and my Yoni already knew each other well and had established their own relationship. Sometimes, he would approach her better than I could.

He began by massaging my whole body and when it was time he asked: "Can I touch your Yoni?" I nodded. My eyes were shut. I wasn't tense. I trusted him. As he started stroking the lips his fingers were like cubes of ice melting on my Yoni, turning into water and becoming part of it.

A few minutes later he asked, "Can I enter your Yoni?"

"Yes, please," I said with a smile, my eyes still shut.

He slipped his finger in. It didn't hurt at all. I felt a tickling sensation when he pressed a certain spot, which opened me up even more, followed by a laughing fit. Every place he touched me made me laugh. It went on like that for over half an hour. I understand why they say that the female orgasm has no end. Every time I reached a climax, another level opened and I could go deeper. I felt ecstatic pleasure. The facilitators told all the couples to finish up and Alon prepared to come out of my Yoni.

"Wait," I said, still giggling, "a little more."

He stayed for two more minutes and then prepared to leave again.

"Please, a little more." I opened my eyes and looked at him.

He smiled at me. "We have to finish," he said.

"Wait, just a little more."

He continued for a few more minutes, staying inside me after all the other couples had already finished and the women were relaxing with their eyes closed.

The facilitators signaled to Alon that it was time to finish up and he said: "I'm going to pull out, love." He withdrew his fingers, placed one hand on my Yoni and the other on my heart. We looked at each other. I would have let him stay inside me for many more hours. I thought back to our Yoni ceremony with Rachel, how we had fought and frozen throughout it. And now, Alon was exploring my Yoni as if he had always known how. Could pregnancy expand pleasure? Or was it the animal through which I was learning to surrender myself?

I RETURNED HOME FROM THE WORKSHOP IN A BETTER MOOD, but I still had a hard time getting out of bed in the morning and through the day. I didn't know when the blues would pass. Some people told me it got better after the first trimester, but I was already in the second. There were days I thought that maybe this was my new and permanent state of being.

In her book *Women Who Run With the Wolves*, Clarissa Pinkola Estés explains that women must enter the darkness within as part of their awakening, but must be careful not to become consumed by the self-destructive forces that exist in us all.

I spoke with two friends who had just returned from the Burning Man festival, and they both told me about orgies, drugs and extreme experiences; but while one was excited and happy, the other sounded broken, confused, and in emotional turmoil. She didn't know what to do with all her experiences. This brought into sharp relief how many people I knew, myself included, were preoccupied with themselves. We had too much time at our disposal and often got lost, carried away to places of lust and confusion, while leaving ourselves behind. It reminded me of the sin of the golden calf. We move from one thrill to the next, from workshop to festival to rave, seeking to feel alive and free. But maybe we were searching in the wrong places?

One day, alone in bed, I felt the familiar pang of desperation: the feeling that the resources available to me were insufficient, that I didn't have anyone to blame or anywhere to run. I reached out for my phone and just before picking it up, stopped myself. It was a moment of choice, not to be sucked into my screen. Just then, Alon came into the room. I turned and greeted him. He sat down next to me on the bed and put his hand on my shoulder.

"I have an idea," he said. "Let's pretend to be therapist and patient. You'll be my patient and we'll see where it goes from there."

I agreed and left the room for a few minutes. When I returned I saw that Alon had spread a white sheet on the floor, lit candles, changed into a white T-shirt and boxers and was sitting with his eyes closed. I sat down opposite him. He slowly opened his eyes, as if he had been living in a temple his whole life, smiled and said in a soft, new-age voice: "How are you, Narkis? Let's start with a brief meditation."

We closed our eyes. At one point, Alon tapped my shoulder, signaling that we were done, and I opened my eyes.

"So, how are you?" he asked again, and I answered with all sincerity, as if I really was being treated by this man. I shared how hard things were, how desperate I felt, as if everything was closing in on me. Every day I woke up to a variation of the same despair. I told him that even after the workshop, which had lifted me a little, I was afraid of being stuck in this state, and didn't know why it wasn't getting better. I was already in my third trimester, and afraid my pregnancy would be harmed, that my despair would destroy everything I had built in life and that I wouldn't be able to function.

Alon listened silently while looking at me. After a long while I realized that he wasn't going to say anything and I concluded, "I'm tired of hearing myself speak. I need another dimension, access to other sources of strength. Maybe you could help me dance?"

Smiling, Alon stood up and walked over to the corner of the room, connected his phone to the speaker and put on some tribal music. Letting the music carry me along its stream, I stood up, waved my hands around and started making strange faces. At one point I lay down on the sofa and continued to dance; and while dancing, I stroked myself, licked myself, bit myself softly, as if I was a jungle animal.

The more I went with the flow, the more sources of energy appeared. The sounds I made were my way of drawing energy from underneath me, from the ground. No meditation, no closing of eyes and evoking a mantra—just licking my whole body, going wild and moving incessantly. My surrender deepened: the animal moved my limbs and I let her do with me as she pleased. I felt alive, I felt animal, the animal I am.

At one point I opened my eyes and saw Alon looking at me. I know when Alon is turned on, his eyes have a different expression. He couldn't understand what I was doing, but it excited him and he started stroking me gently, all over my body. As "therapist" he wasn't supposed to touch me, but offer me a space without an agenda. That said, it was a game to him, and I was his wife after all. He started moving his body while sitting next to me and stroking me. Gradually his movements increased, to the point of him trying to climb on top of me and join in my dance.

"I know I'm your therapist," he said, "but I'm allowing myself to cross the line because I feel like we knew each other in a previous incarnation."

I found it so funny, having a therapist dish up this lame excuse, and thought how fickle, dangerous and stupid new-agey logic can be, as if everything could be explained by some theory. I couldn't stop laughing.

Alon got off the sofa and started dancing in front of me. I got up too. I could see he was in his animal guise, the animal inside him that I'm usually afraid of, that I suppress, that I instruct: "More slowly, gently, not now, not there, not like that." But this time I was also connected to the animal in me. I could look him in the eye, meet him in that place, and contain the man he was.

We started dancing together and making love with our clothes on. Once in a while we drew apart to the same with ourselves, before reconnecting and picking up where we had left off. We moved constantly from the bedroom to the kitchen and living room, letting the music and movement lead us.

Meeting Alon next to the sofa, I took off his pants and danced him around the room. I was turned on, especially by how he was looking at me. I could feel how much he desired me. I understood him, and wished I could always be that way. Everything was so alive, sensual, open, reserves of terrestrial energy radiating life's pleasures. Without drugs, without alcohol, just the two of us together.

I recalled the sex magic ceremony and told him:

"Now think fast — what do you want? The sky is the limit. Come, let's use the orgasmic power to bring something into being."

Alon thought for a moment, smiling and dancing away.

"I want an easy birth and a healthy baby," I said.

"Yes!" Alon cheered me on. And added: "I'm healthy, I'm happy. That's what I want, that's what I want to bring into being."

Alon bent over and began kissing me while I was dancing. I totally surrendered myself to it. The energy flowed from my buttocks to my head — it felt as if the animal was making my spine dance.

I STARTED PERFORMING A SIMILAR CEREMONY EVERY MORNING. To the background of tribal music, I danced like an animal in front of the mirror while making sounds and expressions. Sometimes, when I felt out of sorts or on the brink of depression again, I'd stop everything in the middle of the day, slip away to a private place, put on some music, dance, make noises and faces, bite myself softly, speak gibberish and laugh out loud. Each encounter filled me with energy and vitality.

It also introduced more efficiency to my professional life. I made contact with the animal before a presentation or a workshop, and the encounter would allow me to step on the stage with bright eyes. Prior to this, friends offered support, mostly through motivational talks, which offered only temporary relief. Despite their good intentions, these words only reinforced my mind loops. The connection with the visceral circumvented the loops. I was turned on and fired up.

Not long after the animal had already become part of my daily ritual, we had our monthly *Double You* community meeting. The circle I led was "how to stay turned on." It was almost full. Some participants mentioned needing to rediscover what turned them on after giving birth. Some shared how important it was to initiate sex with their partner, and encouraged each other by forming a WhatsApp group for sharing when they did. Some spoke about exercises they practiced to give them energy and vitality. When it was my turn, I told them about the visceral character that enters me and about the exercise that turns me on. I told them about how it had saved me from the hormonal depression I was suffering from.

"Most people spend a lifetime repressing the animal, putting it in a cage, but this animal doesn't only exhibit embarrassing behavior, it also does good and important things. It is in charge of our creativity, our passion in life. When it's locked up, we sacrifice a large portion of our life energy, of who we are. It's like scheduling a tete-a-tete with the monster inside."

"I know it sounds really strange," I added. "But give it a try—invent an exercise of your own, a practice that renews the carnal energy and connects you with your power every day. It's fine if it feels bizarre at first. Your version has to come from a deep place and won't necessarily be something that others understand."

They listened. Even if some found it bizarre, they were simultaneously intrigued. Iris said that what I was talking about sounded like Kundalini Awakening, and described discovering how working with her breath and certain positions could also be sexually arousing. When it was Shira's turn, she said in a sad and quiet voice that it didn't matter what personal exercise she did, because she and her partner were lost, and their sexuality had come to a standstill.

"The truth is that we're in serious trouble," she said with tears in her eyes. "If we don't solve it, I don't know how we'll stay together. We barely have sex, and when we finally do, something doesn't flow. And I've never had an orgasm with him."

Some of the participants shifted in discomfort, others leaned in and wanted to know more: Was it always like this? How is the communication between you two apart from the sex? Did you have a similar experience with other partners? And other questions.

At one point I asked: "Have you considered going to a workshop or seeking therapy?"

"I want to, but he won't do it," she replied.

"Sounds familiar," I said. "I know how frustrating it can be, but I don't agree that practicing yourself won't make a difference.

Problems in sexuality are usually related to both parties, and so even if only *you* undergo a process, it can lead to a huge improvement in bed."

"What do you mean? How can I do any of this without him?"

"In my own case, it required an intense personal journey towards my femininity. Only then could I enter a process with Alon. The significance goes beyond orgasms or how your partner treats you — it starts with how you treat your body. Without my problems with sexuality, I wouldn't have met the animal inside of me, for example, and then I wouldn't have learned what it means to be a woman."

"I'm not sure I follow," said Shira. "What does it mean, to be a woman?"

"It's a good question... I'm only starting to understand it myself," I admitted. "The one thing I can say with certainty is that it means a lot."

CHAPTER 7
PRESENT WOMEN

"I stand on the sacrifices of a million women before me thinking what can I do to make this mountain taller so the women after me can see farther."

Rupi Kaur

WHEN I WAS SEVEN MONTHS PREGNANT, A GOOD FRIEND OF MINE TOLD ME ABOUT THE IDEA OF ORGASMIC BIRTH, during which something akin to sexual pleasure is experienced. I immediately googled the term, watched documentaries and read blogs in which people shared their orgasmic birth stories. The more I read, the more sense it made. After all, we had conceived as a result of sexual pleasure and I had invested so much into connecting to my body to experience that. Could I also experience pleasure while giving birth, birth being the culmination of the sexual act?

I discovered that there were women around the world who were teaching this, and one of the leaders in the field was an Israeli named Ayala. I read through her homepage. Ayala's definition of orgasmic birth was: "A birth in which at least in some of the contractions there is a physical sensation of pleasure in part or all of the body, which is not the result of physical stimulation or touch."

In her view, giving birth was first and foremost a sexual event and a woman can experience birth the way she experiences lovemaking: she can be attentive and surrender herself to her body, lose control, wander between the physical and other realms. Sounded good to me.

I signed up for her online course. Every week I did the exercises. At first, I was excited about the possibility of experiencing sexual pleasure while giving birth, but soon something deeper hit home. The process of preparation and learning felt like a natural continuation of the sexuality workshops.

In preparation for the birth, there were physical, emotional, spiritual and mental components to the course. We connected to the ideal image of giving birth and released our expectation of going through it. We connected with the embryo, recited a daily prayer blessing the birthing process, and engaged in physical work, such as a Yoni massage, which Alon and I were already familiar with. But the most significant aspect of the course was working with fear.

I was afraid the hospital medical staff would intervene and that I would become anxious, which could obstruct the birth and endanger the baby. The thought alone was alarming. After a few weeks of practicing, I slowly released my fears, performed gratitude exercises for the doctors and midwives, and surrendered to the unknown.

Fortunately, Ayala agreed to be present at the birth and, after visiting a few hospitals, we decided on Ichilov.

IN HIGH SCHOOL, I WAS A LITTLE JEALOUS OF PEOPLE WHO HAD BEEN IN CAR ACCIDENTS AND RECOVERED. It wasn't a penchant for morbidity, but the desire to live better. Reading interviews with people who had suffered severe illnesses or accidents showed me how these experiences had forced them to slow down, look at their lives, realize what was truly important, and to alter the status quo.

I was seeking a turning point that would be imposed on me from without, and that would force me to respect myself: my body, my needs, my rhythm, my **real** dreams. Looking back, you could say that my car accident was giving birth.

5:05

Awake on and off during the night with contractions. I woke Alon and we started timing them. Trying to catch some sleep in between, I shut my eyes, listened to music and felt myself gradually disappear. It felt really good.

16:20

Ayala comes to visit. She says this is a good time to rest, to reach every contraction in a state of relaxation and to work on breathing. Meditation in between is also an option. She says there is no such thing as time, it's an illusion, and to just let myself be in this moment. My body is working on bringing my baby into the world and I have to focus fully on that. That is what matters. I have permission to stop time.

16:39

Timing the contractions is strange. I wish I could connect to my body in a way that would let me know how far along I am without timing them.

20:43

Ayala came over again. She taught me how to move while having contractions and explained why I should get up when I'm having one. She assured me that it was fine if it took a few more days. No pressure. She was there for almost three hours, we sang songs, had deep conversations and grew closer. I'm surrendering myself to it. I can feel it.

00:30

During contractions I utter helpful and encouraging statements such as: "This pain is like the act of creation that is now opening me so that our child can come forth"; or: "Every contraction is a wave that has a painful peak, but the beginning and the end are fine."

5:28

At night, I spent a few hours in the bath listening to hypnobirthing meditations that guided me to breathe deeply and imagine the baby sliding out peacefully. At a particularly painful point, I set the New Age mantras and meditations aside and the beloved inner animal came to my aid. Succumbing to its roar I finally connected to my power, Alon and I started a love session, which involved a few minutes of hugging and intimacy; during a contraction I would stand up, make animal noises and return to him.

Sleep is not a possibility. It's like I'm stuck in my body.

6:40

At Ichilov Hospital. It's not easy. Sitting together outside the emergency room, I cried and asked the universe for help. Later the doctor performed a membrane sweep. We decided to go back home, continue with the contractions there, and return when the birth had advanced. In the meantime, the contractions were growing stronger. Every few minutes I'd take a moment to scream and howl through a painful one, like a cat in heat, and then go back to writing or being with Alon.

What a mystery birth is.

8:21

Strangely enough, it feels good. Alon and I are lying at home in our bed, resting between contractions. Every few minutes I growl and let the contraction pass through me. In between there is gratitude and I do my best not to anticipate the next contraction and instead behave like someone who's resting. Everything that's happening is so exciting. Is this the pleasure Ayala was referring to? The contractions themselves are the most painful, un-pleasurable sensations I've ever experienced.

But Alon's support is so moving. I start crying and launch into a monologue: "You're the most amazing person I know. I don't know anyone like you. You time my contractions so perfectly. You're going to be such an amazing father. You're so thorough," I marvel. My sentences are punctuated by sobs. In the fourth sentence, Alon joins in and we both hug and sob in bed. Every few minutes I stand up for the contraction, and in between it feels so good and special. Truly life itself.

How beautiful — the screams, the sobs — the way the heart opens up.

Ayala arrived at around 9:00 a.m. The house was dark apart from some candles burning and music playing in the background, like in the sexuality temples. I was in bed. Ayala gave me a massage between contractions, and with each one tried to help me breathe and release low, deep sounds, while also helping me stand up to experience the contraction leaning on pillows instead of lying down.

Between contractions I felt good. I rested, songs played in the background, Ayala and Alon gave me massages. With the arrival of each contraction my body was racked with pain. Only that moment existed. When a moment is full of pain, there is only pain; when it is full of relief, there is relief. And so, like an animal in nature, I moved through the sharp transitions between pain and feeling good.

At one point I fell apart. I told Ayala: "I'm weak, I thought it would be the kind of pain I could rise above, but I can't. I can't rise above the contractions."

She looked into my eyes and said gently: "Honey, you're not supposed to rise above anything right now. On the contrary. You're supposed to go as low as possible." That sentence opened my birth. I let myself get low — I didn't only act like an animal, I actually became the animal. My thoughts were replaced with growling, and I became more and more my own body. I noticed Alon whisper something to Ayala. A few minutes later Ayala said: "Let's go to the hospital."

I wasn't sure I was dilated enough to give birth. Maybe I was still in that latent phase that would last forever. It was a little like what I had felt in the Ayahuasca, stuck in a reality I had no control over. It was clear to me they were right and that it was time to go to the hospital.

It was a beautiful sunny day. The drive did me good. I sat in the back with Ayala who supported me through every contraction. She held my hands and vocalized my pain with me. There was traffic. I concentrated on the contractions and wasn't worried about when we'd get there — something inside me knew everything would work out.

In the delivery room they tried to hook me up to the monitor, but I screamed that I needed water on my body and, as is becoming of an animal, I detached myself from the monitor and ran to the bathroom. I sat down on the toilet and Ayala sprayed my stomach with the shower head. The pain died down and the lovely midwife hooked me up to a wireless monitor.

It was in the hospital, of all places, from the toilet seat in the delivery room, where release came. I surrendered to the contractions, screamed through each one and no longer felt sorry for myself. I wasn't thinking anymore. I remember Alon looking at me and crying out of excitement, and myself marveling that this was the father of the baby that was about to come out of me. At one point, they told us the natural delivery room was available, but it seemed impossible to leave where I was, so I said I didn't want it.

Ayala looked at me skeptically. "You want it. Trust me. You need the Jacuzzi there and you want that room," she stressed.

My animal instinct took over, and decided: this woman has been a great help to me. I'll listen to her.

After a few minutes in the natural delivery room I screamed: "My pelvis! My pelvis!"

"You seem to be pushing," the midwife said. She examined me. I was fully dilated.

"There is no doubt that something has moved downward," said Ayala.

The contractions that contained the urge to push were accompanied by excruciating pain.

Alon began to shout: "Our baby is about to come out! Our baby is about to come out of your body!"

"I'm breaking your water," I heard the midwife say. A huge wave of energy rushed over me and… silence. Followed by a cry.

The moment they placed him on me, Lavie stopped crying. They couldn't get me to stop moving in order to stitch my vaginal opening, so, after a completely natural birth, they took me into an operating room and anesthetized me for two simple stitches.

Giving birth was the hardest thing my body had ever been through. It was also difficult afterwards. They tried to explain breastfeeding, but I didn't understand. How could more demands be made from my body after three days without sleep?

At home, my daily animal ritual was replaced by a healing ceremony for my broken body. I would shower, lie down naked on the bed, spread my legs, spray my Yoni with Aloe Vera without looking and with as little touching as possible. The stitches still hurt. Then I'd shut my eyes, place my hands a few centimeters above my Yoni and say to her: "Thank you. You sacrificed a lot allowing Lavie to be born. Thank you for healing, thank you for being flexible. I love you."

Then I'd move my hands further up, place them on my lower abdomen, where my womb was gradually shrinking, and say, "Thank you for helping Lavie grow so beautifully in these past few months, thank you for returning to your original size and place. I love you." Then I would move my hands up to my breasts, which were huge, and say to them: "Thank you for producing milk for Lavie and feeding him. Thank you, nipple, for letting his mouth latch on to you and allowing him to be fed." Finally, I would place my hands on my heart and say: "Thank you for being strong. I love you. Thank you for giving me comfort."

After the ritual, I'd call Alon. I would spread my legs and he would take a photo of my still-swollen Yoni. We would look at it together, compare the picture from that day with the one from a few days before. I'd usually burst into tears and snuggle up close to my beloved neck. From day to day, my Yoni became less swollen and my body less broken.

AFTER THREE MONTHS OF BEING PARENTS, WE SPENT MOST OF OUR TIME TALKING ABOUT MONEY. These conversations created a lot of tension between us. On paper we were privileged, but our bank account was always in overdraft, and now there was a baby in the picture. It wasn't a game anymore.

I'd imagine us not being able to pay the rent and feel stressed. I knew that most of it derived from not knowing what I was actually going to do now to make a living. Should I continue focusing on Double You? Start a new project? Provide additional consultations? Ever since the birth I was pulling indecisively in all directions.

One morning, after I had finished breastfeeding and Lavie stopped fussing, I managed to fall asleep again. At one point, I realized I was in a dream, a lucid dream— asleep but aware of being in a dream. After the birth this ability intensified. It was probably the combination of open consciousness and waking up several times each night because of Lavie — this alternating wakefulness and sleep was conducive to lucid dreaming.

In the past, when I had a lucid dream, I'd want to fly or reach the moon, before coming to realize it was just an opportunity to better know myself and gain another perspective on life.

On that lucid dream night, I asked: "What should I do in life? What should I work at?"

Immediately I saw a painting of a woman. It was intriguing, if indistinct: she seemed like a tormented human-animal whose body was linked to the whole of creation. Through her I suddenly beheld spectacular natural landscapes: green meadows with white flowers, half-bright, half-cloudy skies, and a defined, pleasant breeze to which the grass swayed.

I started moving as if tethered to the wind. I was one with nature. High frequencies washed over my body. Zooming out, I felt as if I was being taken farther and farther upwards until I could see Earth from the outside. At one point it became a bit scary; even though I knew it was a dream, the experience of seeing Earth from above was too much for me. After the Ayahuasca I had learned my lesson regarding situations that challenge my consciousness, so I asked the dream to change scenes.

I segued to a small water reserve surrounded by rocks. The water was clear and cool. People were busy doing their own thing. Suddenly, I wondered whether Alon was there with me and remembered that I was in the midst of a lucid dream. Alon emerged from behind a boulder. He leaned against it and I leaned against him. We held hands and he kissed my neck. I noticed Lavie was also there with us. In the dream, I let him play alone in the water, even though he was only three months old, but then he started to whimper so I went to pick him up. The three of us were together. A family.

I woke to the sound of Lavie, who was completely awake. I looked at my clock. It felt like a long time had passed but it had been less than fifteen minutes. I thought about the dream and the question that had motivated the experience: "What should I do now in life?" In a way, Alon and I were also living in a dream, an illusion we needed to wake up from, or at least direct toward places that meshed with the narrative we wanted to live.

How can we connect to nature? How can we leave the Matrix and stop thinking about money all day long?

IN THE MONTHS THAT FOLLOWED THE BIRTH, I DISTANCED MYSELF FROM MY BODY AND SEXUALITY. A picture that intermittently came to mind those days was from the scene in The Matrix in which Neo is shown that human energy is being used to keep the agents alive. Humans were trapped in capsules living in a virtual reality, images shifting in their consciousness in an existence based on avoiding suffering and pursuing pleasure.

In no small way, I had also placed myself in a capsule that fed my consciousness with changing images posing as life. I had already experienced what it felt like to be present inside my body, and it was hard for me to ignore the fact that my body had become somewhat numb.

Following the lucid dream, I decided to return to my daily practice with the animal and reconnect with my body. However, now as a post-partum woman — lacking sexual desire or the ability to plan my life, I was mainly interested in catching up on sleep. My encounters with the animal developed accordingly. While pleasuring myself, instead of engaging in distant fantasies involving surrender or unfulfilled dreams, I'd touch my Yoni gently, without any sudden movements or conjuring any particular image, as though calling to my soul: Come, come, let's land here. Come and express yourself.

From one day to the next, while my Yoni tingled, I felt more parts returning and my body filling with energy that flowed through it like a river. Flowing beyond the fears, beyond the addiction, beyond the despair and lack of sleep. My tiredness was replaced by curiosity, my anger by inspiration and possibility. I was part of one loving energy. On a psychedelic trip of my own making. A mother inside a body that had given birth. Full of a desire to create and a willingness to meet life where it is.

Within a few weeks of getting back to my body, I found the energy and passion with which to embrace productivity. That's when the "present women" arrived. That's what I called them. When I left the house in the morning, I suddenly came across them everywhere, one after the other. It wasn't clear if I had summoned them into my life or if they had always been there, and only now I was able to notice them: These Present Women.

SARA TANCMAN IS THE FOUNDER OF KEREN BRIAH, a feminist health organization whose goal is to change the way the health system treats women. The organization had already made some comprehensive changes, among them, the way a gynecological examination takes place in Israel (for example, women must be offered a sheet to cover themselves and informed of what the examination will entail, etc.).

When Sara was five months pregnant with twins, she went to her obstetrician and reported that she wasn't feeling well.

"Pregnant women are hysterical. Everything's fine. Go home," the doctor said.

That day Sara had a stillbirth. Soon afterwards, she decided to establish the organization.

The moment I heard her story, I asked to volunteer and become a board member. At the annual board meeting we reviewed a report that presented the non-profit's performance, expenses and planning versus execution. I ate a lot of snacks and doodled on a piece of paper. 'I'm bored,' I thought to myself. 'I hate meetings. That's why I never wanted to get into politics. What have I gotten myself into?' At one point, something in the room woke me up.

Sara was speaking about fundraising. She wasn't good at it but the organization needed more money to accomplish even a fraction of what they had set out to do. Sara dedicated all her time to the non-profit, without a salary. This was her life's work. She managed the non-profit professionally and honestly.

Whenever anyone talks about money, I wake up.

"How much do you need?" I asked.

She cringed. "400,000 shekels."

I started suggesting donors, and Sara shuddered. The meeting had lasted for more than two hours and everyone started packing up. Now they were leaving?

"If we're not discussing this today," I said, "let's continue by phone in the next few days, since this is, after all, the most important topic."

Tamar, who helps women familiarize themselves with their menstrual cycle, was sitting on the other side of the table. She wasn't happy to end on that note. "Let's not end the meeting like this. Sara. Even if you aren't able to raise more money, what you're accomplishing is beautiful and important. Even if we continue at the same pace, it's amazing and you should be proud of yourself."

What she said put me off even more.

"No," I disagreed. "Why do we always do this?" I was referring to the female sex. "We settle for less, for a slow pace, for what we're comfortable dealing with. What we're doing here is vital, and we need to grow faster and help more people. Why do only men know how to fundraise? It's time we also move money around and build things in the world. This tendency we have as women to say 'never mind' and 'we'll manage' stems from oppression!"

"That's not true," said Tamar, "it comes from estrogen. We have estrogen and that's vital. It's the most beautiful thing in the world and we have to use it."

I wasn't sure what she meant. I knew that estrogen was a hormone that was somehow linked to the menstrual cycle, but I didn't know how it affected our temperament. I could only imagine.

"Sara, you're amazing," I continued. "You're an exceptional leader, doing much-needed work, and you deserve resources. I'd be happy to put you in touch with philanthropic funds and people I know." But I could see it wasn't getting through. She was still cringing. And then I had an idea. Followed by butterflies. Really? I asked myself. I waited a few seconds while they summed up the meeting, then took a deep breath and said: "Sara, I know it's not much, but the important thing is the intention. I'll get you started, with 10,000 shekels. If I had more, I'd give more."

Immediately, her body language changed. Her shoulders loosened, and hands widened. She was surprised. Everyone was surprised. It's amazing how the atmosphere changes in a room when someone moves from talk to action.

"You're amazing," I continued, "and I want you to know that. I want this to serve as a reminder of that," I said and started crying. And then Sara started crying. And Tamar too. Everyone in the room was tearful. The estrogen had kicked in and we all melted.

It took me five years and one birth to transform from someone who tells an employee that breastfeeding is no excuse to be late for a meeting to emanating conference-room decorum based on compassion and hormones. I felt that these women came from a future I was still trying to get accustomed to.

The Buddha said, "When the student is ready, the teacher will appear." Sure enough, a few weeks later, I met Luna.

WHEN LAVIE WAS SIX MONTHS OLD, I PUMPED MILK, asked for help from Alon and our mothers, and got on a plane. It was our first time apart. I had accepted an invitation to speak at a Nexus Conference in New York and planned the shortest trip I could — four days, including the flights.

Nexus is a global network that links up social entrepreneurs, philanthropists and investors under forty. The organization encourages collaboration between young leaders to promote global social projects and informal humanitarian aid between countries. At this convention, I would be conducting an on-stage interview, in front of 700 people, with Anne-Marie Slaughter, who had worked for Hilary Clinton and was Director of Policy Planning for the U.S. State Department. This was one of the women I most admired in the area of promoting a policy of work/life balance.

As part of my role at the convention, I also would be joining a roundtable discussion at the U.N. on the topic of sexual harassment in the workplace. That meeting took place the day I landed. I was jetlagged and my breasts ached from pumping.

I got out of the taxi rolling a suitcase, wearing a black suit, high-heels and a Chanel bag — clothes I had borrowed from Sarah, my business partner. I looked up and gazed at the U.N. buildings. How beautiful it is here, I thought, like in the movies. The world's flags waved on the poles opposite skyscrapers with guarded gates. Looking around, I saw a number of buildings with the U.N. logo, but wasn't sure which one was the right one. The meeting was starting in an hour.

Yesimi Juliana Luna is a Brazilian entrepreneur, also in her thirties, who helps women reach self-fulfillment by connecting to their menstrual cycles. Most people call her Luna ("moon"). We had gotten to know each other a few years earlier, when she came to Israel as part of a delegation of entrepreneurs, and this time had arranged to meet before the roundtable. While searching for the café, someone clasped my shoulders.. Luna was gorgeous: curly hair, sculpted face, glasses over almond-colored eyes and a yellow dress (amazing — why hadn't I worn yellow?). We hugged.

We walked into the café arm in arm, as if we were a couple. The guy at the entrance looked at us strangely but we smiled and walked on. It seemed as if Luna felt at home anywhere she went.

We sat down at a table and after two minutes of "how are you" and "what's up," Luna started: "OK, we don't have much time. I need you to see this model I've learned. It isn't new information, it's always been here, we just have to make it accessible to the women we support."

Luna took a pencil and notebook out of her bag, tore off a page, drew a circle on it and divided it into four. "I don't know if you know this, but as women, we are a part of nature, just like the seasons," she said. "Every month, the process that happens in nature occurs in our bodies as well." Luna spoke in a low voice, as if she was sharing a secret.

"You mean our menstrual cycle?"

"Yes. It's not just a matter of the days we bleed, it's our cycle in general: every day of the month has significance. If you synchronize yourself with it, your life will change. Suddenly you'll realize that your changing moods don't mean you're crazy, but that they are part of an awe-inspiring process."

Luna drew the ovulation on one side and the period on the other.

"Let's start big," she said. "Think about the fact that the days you bleed are the days you were supposed to get pregnant, but didn't. Nature would want you to rest if you were pregnant, to take care of the embryo developing inside you. So these are days we want to stay at home. Our mood is low, but during these days we have access to deep sources inside ourselves, to ideas, insights, completion of internal processes.

"Ovulation is the time you can get pregnant—and when nature wants you to get out of the house and find a partner. These are days when we want to meet people and appear in public. It's an excellent time for being active. Your period and ovulation are the two extreme axis points of this process, and each day between them has its unique character."

"Each day?"

"Yes, every day more abilities present themselves and your body directs you to synchronize with it. If you are in sync, the forces of nature will be with you. If you resist, you struggle against nature itself. All this information is in your panties. There are some days without discharge, some days with discharge that isn't fertile, and days when it is fertile, wet and smooth. It's not relevant only to a physical pregnancy but also to a spiritual one. During the month, pay attention to the right and wrong times for meeting people—when you're better being with yourself and your reflections and when you want to get out and take on the world. If you monitor it every month for a whole quarter, you'll notice a clear pattern. For example, where are you in your menstrual cycle today?"

"Actually, I have no idea. I'm nursing and haven't bled in months."

"Makes no difference. Even if you don't get your period you still have your cycle. You can find out easily. I'll show you." She pulled out another page and asked me to document my feelings from the past few days, so that she could help me locate them in the relevant quarter. I started thinking, then stopped to check the time. Oh no, the roundtable was in twenty minutes and I still hadn't pumped any milk.

"Will you come with me while I pump?" I asked Luna while asking where the restrooms were. "The meeting is starting soon."

"Sure," she replied.

I sat down on the toilet lid, took out the pump, and connected it to the electrical socket and my breast. With the sound of pumping in the background, I shared my feelings from the last few days.

Luna sat on the floor and wrote everything down. When I was finished speaking, I switched to the other breast and Luna showed me where I was in my monthly cycle.

"You're in the quarter that comes after ovulation. These are the days our energy reserves are low. Some women even feel a little down, from forcing their bodies to behave in a way they're not meant to at this time of the month." Luna gave me a few tips, such as making sure I get enough alone time even though I'm at the convention, even if it means going to the bathroom for twenty minutes, or not getting straight out of bed in the morning. She taught me breathing exercises to help me connect with my body and explained which foods are recommended for each part of the cycle. "Start monitoring how you feel every day from now on," she concluded. "If you do it for three months, you'll see that the feelings repeat themselves every month. This way you'll have a clearer understanding of your cycle and can plan your days accordingly. Try it and let me know how it goes."

"That's it?"

"I give a whole course on it, but we don't have time. Get started. You'll be surprised to discover how simpler life becomes when we're in sync with our cycle."

Outside the bathroom a woman in a suit who was waiting gave us a strange look — what were we doing in there together? Luna and I smiled. We said goodbye and agreed to continue our conversation online. My head held high, I marched over to the meeting hall.

WE SAT AROUND A LONG CONFERENCE ROOM TABLE, flags behind us and pens and paper at the ready for a brainstorming session. At the head of the table sat a U.N. representative with graying hair, probably in his fifties, who seemed empathetic.

At the start of the meeting, he explained the U.N.'s point of view regarding sexual harassment in the workplace. He declared that they know they don't know and were searching for creative solutions that would come from our generation. Originally, I had planned to keep a low profile at this meeting, because I was afraid of saying the wrong thing and to never be invited again, but my conversation with Luna had given me courage. She reminded me that our authentic voice as women needed to be heard.

When he finished speaking, we began the roundtable discussion. I wrote down all the points in my notebook to organize my thoughts. While writing I started getting butterflies in my stomach. Here I was, in one of the most distinguished places in the world, preparing to propose that in order to solve the problem of sexual harassment, women and men had to make peace through their sexuality in the workplace itself.

When it was my turn I said the following:

"The #MeToo movement brought to light an unfortunate reality: Western society has turned men and women into enemies. I believe that the main reason for this derives from the way men and women are encouraged to repress the fact that they are sexual beings. But sexuality shouldn't be taboo. The more we try to sweep it under the rug, the more it will resurface.

"Much like feelings or thoughts, sexuality is an inseparable part of who we are and constitutes a significant part of the communication between us. In order to improve the dialogue between men and women and create a safe working environment, we need programs that will teach appropriate sexual conduct. Today workplaces only teach us what inappropriate sexual conduct is, and all these programs appear to have been written by lawyers.

"But we're talking about human beings: men and women need to know how to manage their sexual energy, learn their boundaries and communicate them in a healthy way. Women have to feel comfortable in their bodies, comfortable saying 'no,' being dominant. Men have to feel comfortable expressing emotion, being vulnerable and containing feminine power.

"We have been taught that these behaviors put us at risk of seeming weak or not being taken seriously, but until we raise this topic in the workplace, the struggle between men and women will continue and we're all already paying the price.

"Practices and exercises supporting such a process already exist in the world of healthy sexuality. The time has arrived to adapt this knowledge to the workplace. It would be sufficient to introduce the foundation exercises from these workshops, some of which we have already introduced to a small number of organizations, to bring about a real revolution in the communication and balance of power between men and women in the workplace."

The butterflies settled down. The U.N. representative thanked me, and said he liked the idea of creating another type of intervention program that would teach "sexual conduct," and was eager to hear more. When we summarized the meeting, he asked us to create a team to continue developing this topic.

Afterwards, one of the participants walked up to me and introduced herself.

"Hi, nice to meet you, my name is Katherin. I'd like to join the team working on the program, I have a lot to say about this topic. On paper, what you said is nice, but it sounds naïve," she said, somewhat aggressively, while organizing her bag.

"What's naïve about it?" I asked, looking straight into her eyes, inviting her to be with me for a moment.

"To think that implementing a program in the workplace will help men and women reach harmony on their way to some utopian existence with love and glitter. I work with victims of sexual assault and am one myself. It's only in the last few years that awareness of all the wrongs men have done to women has finally started to grow. We're not going to be able to forgive or trust them so fast." She closed her bag and started for the door.

"I've also been working with women for several years, some of whom are also victims. In my opinion we can forgive and trust faster than you say," I called out after her. She turned around. I continued, "We're women. We can bring life into the world, we have estrogen, we get our periods, we are inherently connected to love and can choose it," I said with a smile, still inspired by my conversation with Luna.

Halfway out the door, Katherin replied: "That's also naïve. It's easy for you to say that. Do you have any idea what kind of cases I come across? Love and compassion are a privilege not all of us are lucky enough to possess."

I knew that there was truth to what Katherin was saying. There were such terrible cases, and sometimes speaking with a victim about compassion was like a continuation of the assault against her. That month I had met Marva Zohar, a survivor of a gang rape, who was nothing but love and compassion through and through.

Through Marva I learned that both approaches need to co-exist.

CHAPTER 8
A MAN AND A WOMAN

"Have enough courage to trust love one more time and always one more time."

Maya Angelou

"If I stop for a moment to really consider what the gang rape I endured took away from me, I have to admit: so much. It took away my innate right to discover my sexuality at my own pace. It took away so many moments in which, instead of sleeping at night, or working, or functioning, or fulfilling my dreams, or loving myself and loving men and loving my life, I had no choice but to pick up the pieces."

Marva Zohar was one of the first interviewees on my podcast "Playing with Fire," which I started to create a space where men and women could talk about sexuality and relationships without barriers.

The gang rape Marva experienced as a teenager sent her in pursuit of healing, a process which transformed her into a poet, a midwife and the founder of Amen — a residential trauma treatment program for victims of sexual assault.

We named the episode "Ending the Rape Culture." In it, Marva responded to men's testimonies about why they believed sexual assault against women persists.

In the episode, Dan shared his perspective on the root of the problem. "Ask a man to go for two weeks without sex, just try it. How many men would be able to handle that? It's a tough dependency no one talks about, the pain and dependency men have when it comes to sex. Most men look at the world and believe that women are supposed to satisfy their sexual urges. It is an unspoken pain. There's no room in the world for a man to say 'I'm hurting,' 'I'm having a hard time.' We are a very sick society, and then, when the disease is exposed, everyone lashes out at men: 'they should be castrated,' 'they should be killed.' A second ago you were a victim and now you're the aggressor. It also happens with men who are yearning for love and don't know how to obtain it, and a moment later, it emerges in the form of aggression. The same wound exists in all of us. Our way of coping as men and women is to go on the attack and want to hurt everything. If I told a woman who has been raped—and most women I know have been raped in one way or another—that the man who raped her is no less a victim than she is, I don't think she'd be happy to hear that. Most chances are she would never talk to me again. It's hard to acknowledge that the person who has wounded you is himself wounded."

Marva responded:

"Basically, whoever wounds others is in a sense wounded themselves. Though, statistically speaking, we know that not every rapist comes from a violent home, so it also comes from other places. It's complicated.

"When I was hospitalized for the first time, I saw many women who had injured themselves in various ways: one banged her head against the wall, the other had an eating disorder, another would cut herself. And then I came across a powerful text written by Evelyn Wright, which had a great impact on me. The main idea is that it simply cannot be that the only form of violence or anger permitted to women is self-destruction. So many women feel sorry for their rapists and become confused: we have pity and compassion for them, but not for ourselves, and then we swallow this anger and hurt ourselves to the point of suicide.

"Forgiveness and absolution are certainly the goal, but we cannot skip over the phase of sacred anger. That's one level. But on another, on the spiritual level of what can bring about healing, we are all human beings—we suffer and we hurt each other. Being the aggressor is accompanied by a lot of suffering, I believe that. As a society we certainly must also commit to help heal the aggressors, and part of that is to acknowledge what they have done.

"The very fact that men are violent means they are in great distress. What happens to those men who rape? What sort of dreadful condition do you have to be in to rape?

"I dream of justice and truth committees that will take place one day between men and women, like the committees that took place in South Africa at the end of apartheid, when they realized that the regime was finished and now people had to live together. If a civil war had broken out, that anger would have been perpetuated, without the creation of a new culture or society, and the jails would have been overflowing; and so a process of healing and acknowledging the pain had to get underway. The justice committees were possible because the murderous regime had come to an end, but here the violence continues. How can you speak of forgiveness, absolution and healing when women are still being raped and murdered? I think that in this case it will have to happen simultaneously, the movement of the 'enough, we must put an end to it' and increasing the punishment, while at the same time feeling the pain and talking about it. And listening. Truly listening.

"I want us to have the capacity to cry together over the immense pain, to reach levels of connection that will leave no room for disconnection, because this disconnection is what enables the violence. I want us to really examine the pain that has endured generation after generation. My feeling is that the discourse we have today is limited: either women are guilty, or let's castrate the men, or just let's learn healthy sexuality and everything will be fine. It goes much deeper than that. To effect real change you need to be able to talk, and men are scared to talk for various reasons, not all of which I understand. We have to realize that we are a tribe, a community, that we are together in this. If only we could hear, listen and communicate in a way that would bring us closer.

"Remember: these are not beasts, animals, or monsters. We are all human beings, and if we can figure out how to examine the gray areas of the "almost," that's where the healing can begin. I'd like to inhabit a space that will make room for that discourse, because this problem cannot be solved without the men."

AS PART OF THE PODCAST AND FACEBOOK COMMUNITY I LEAD, "PLAYING WITH FIRE," I had the opportunity to hear and read the testimonials of thousands of men, and as a result began to better understand them. It turns out that men also have complexes surrounding their sexuality. Previously, I was certain that patriarchal society only signaled to women that they should repress their sexuality and distance themselves from their body. I thought that as long as we women continued performing the work of healing from the oppression we have been subjected to, at one point we would be healed and achieve equality.

But now I was thinking — what equality? With whom? The masculinity presented on screen, including, of course, porn, is a distortion. So many men also require a deep healing process to counteract the side effects of this distortion. The patriarchy doesn't spare men; it oppresses them as well. I learned about the scope of hidden depression men suffer, the challenge to recognize and relay their emotions, and the enormous anxieties they harbor because of society's expectation that men provide and be strong.

There appears to be a direct link between our sexual conditioning and the violence that plagues our society: from a young age men are encouraged to act violently, while women are encouraged to contain this violence, a conditioning that has a direct impact on the balance of power between us.

I also learned more about us as women. Given the society in which we live, one of our greatest challenges is to get to know our bodies and respond to their needs, which is why many of us have difficulty reaching an orgasm. Ignoring our bodies doesn't only affect our sexual satisfaction, it also damages our confidence and the way we express ourselves in the world. Ironically, without even noticing, many of us collaborate with the very cultural values that have oppressed us.

The female body was once considered an object, legally regarded as property—and this legacy continues to affect women to this day. Issues such as body image, eating disorders, and the repression of physical needs are all side effects of this historical viewpoint.

I wish that as women, we could invest our resources, both mental and material, in building the world we desire to create. We can lead. And we should. Not instead of men, but alongside them. This is what we are required to do. Now. And no one can do it on our behalf. The healing can come from us, with the support of men but without a dependence on them. We can't influence them while trying to fall in line with the same society that continues to oppress them as well.

These messages are especially important today, as extremists attempt to undermine the progress made by feminist movements and reverse women's rights. The female body was always a weapon in the struggle between conservative and liberal movements. A woman's right to pleasure and bodily autonomy and sovereignty is still being denied in many parts of the world (including in Western countries).

We tend to think that all we need is to influence the policy makers (mostly men), but this is not enough; as long as women continue to buy into the belief that their bodies are objects someone else can decide upon, they will remain vulnerable.

In some countries women still don't have the right to an education, to open a bank account or seek an abortion. This is a troubling and infuriating reality, which is why many feminist movements and their resources have rightly focused on advocacy.

But in addition to hearing our "no," it is time we simultaneously sound our "yes" loud and clear — to define what kind of world we do want to create, not as the result of a struggle, or from finally being granted our freedom, but by creating an alternative ourselves, together. If we want the world to view our ideas as worthy, we must first perceive them as such: to commit to raise funds; pursue our passion projects that until now have been regarded as hobbies; collaborate, work as a team; follow through with our vision; mobilize resources to allow more women to make choices with respect to their relationships, careers, and bodies, which they need to listen to. If we want to change the conversation surrounding the female body, we must know our bodies, explore them, celebrate them, give them the honor they deserve. And it must start with the younger generation, with our daughters.

In my vision, I see girls going through initiation ceremonies when they get their periods, celebrating their cycle with the boys in class, receiving practical tools for working with their cycle, being proud of their femininity! They walk the world knowing that they are happy to be women. The schools and homes where they grow up teach them to listen to the wisdom of their bodies, starting with the way they are bathed as babies, to the manner in which they are spoken to at home; educated to love their sacred body, and know that no one should ever hurt it. And of course, these values should also be instilled in boys in relation to their bodies.

I see men and women working together to heal one another, to maintain a productive dialogue and rise above the conditioning of gender, to fashion a reality in which everyone can find their place. They celebrate the blessing of the body, and the possibility of experiencing pleasure. They know and respect it, treating their own body as a gift and from that perspective touching other people.

I see a world in which men and women who are connected to their body are equally connected to the earth: they respect it, work the land, and make sacrifices to keep it sustainable.

Such a world has the potential to yield not only a full life, but also to lead to peace on Earth: the most important peace of all — between men and women.

SOMEONE ONCE TOLD ME THAT THE WAR BETWEEN MEN AND WOMEN IS THE FINAL AND MOST IMPORTANT WAR THAT HUMAN BEINGS HAVE TO OVERCOME, that if we manage to resolve it — an entirely new reality would exist.

Rabbi Akivah said:

"If man and woman are deserving, God's presence dwells in their midst.

If they are not deserving, fire devours them."

In one week in 2020, amidst reports of yet another woman who had been murdered in Israel, Alon and I were in an argument about a wound in our relationship that had reopened. Basically, what usually happens is that I feel hurt by something Alon said or didn't do for me and, to avoid getting hurt again in the future, I set conditions intended to protect me. In response, Alon accuses me of trying to control him and will not listen to any demands if I make them in anger, and without taking any responsibility.

These issues are usually resolved in one discussion in which we both manage to see each other, but that week we weren't able to. Following the dramatic news, this time it felt as if we were fighting in the name of all the men and all the women who were angry at each other.

After several days of arguing, avoiding contact and limiting our conversation to logistical matters, my anger deepened. One night, lying next to Alon in bed, I noticed that this man was someone I usually felt love for, but at that moment discerned within me only anger and the desire to fight. That week the war between men and women became the theme of my life.

One day, I went to a store to exchange something. I parked on the curb because, due to Covid, customers couldn't come inside. While exchanging my item, a man drove past and through his window shouted: "It's not OK to park like that!" While apologizing and signaling that I would only be another minute, I saw his lips moving, clearly gesturing to me: "Bitch, bitch, bitch, you are a b-i-t-c-h."

Another evening that week, a smart and successful businesswoman that I respect told me proudly: "It's taken me many years, but I've finally decided I never want to work for any man again. I've reached the conclusion that I hate men."

The pinnacle of the week was an investigative news interview I watched with Shira Iskov, who had survived her husband's attempt on her life. Shira described the early indications: he was jealous of her breastfeeding their son; he demanded that she throw away a strapless dress; he kicked and pushed her. While listening and becoming increasingly outraged, I realized that with every detail, my resentment toward the male sex and its representative living in my house grew — Alon, despite him being a very respectful partner and having nothing to do with the circle of violence.

For a number of days Alon and I stuck to our guns, unwilling to hear or understand anything, and everything we saw outside reinforced the polarity inside, at home. On the weekend, having grown weary of rehashing the same arguments, we realized that we probably wouldn't reach an understanding through words. It was time to let our bodies take over.

So, we made love and something happened that made no sense, that transcended logic: the moment Alon was inside me, I looked into his eyes and understood something of his anger. I saw how the walls I had erected were hurting him and preventing communication. For the first time in a week, I felt he also saw me and my anger toward the male sex. While we were making love, I also had another revelation about the significance of penetration, the connection of the sex organs, the consent to come together. All was built in the act itself or destroyed in its absence.

When I pulled Alon's body out of mine, he was confused. I smiled at him.

"I want us to stop for a moment and perform a ceremony," I said.

I immediately looked down at his Lingam, avoiding eye contact.

"I would like to bless you," I said, "for your life force, your vitality, for being the driving force in bringing our son Lavie into the world." I gave his penis loving kisses and then raised my eyes to meet his. Alon had a surprised expression on his face. Even for me, this was a sudden move.

I smiled at him and carried on: I blessed his behind, his stomach, his pure heart, his neck, his mouth, his eyes, eyelashes. I licked his ears and then returned to his Lingam and continued giving it love.

At one point Alon stopped me and moved my body so that we switched positions. Now he seemed relaxed and amused by the situation. I realized he had decided to partake of the ceremony (already used to the fact that our life had become a workshop).

He started blessing me in response, caressing my uterus and thanking her, "Thank you for nurturing Lavie inside you, thank you for bringing this beloved child into our lives."

He stroked my Yoni and blessed her too: "Thank you for being so open. Thank you for being magical."

I felt vibrations rising along my spine and I melted into the mattress.

At one point, I invited him to come back in. The sensation was very different, the anger had passed, I was open to him. We moved gently together. I moved from pleasure to pleasure. With every passing moment it felt better and better. At one point I disappeared in this lovemaking as if we were one body.

I SUDDENLY REALIZED THAT I WAS HAVING SEX WITH MY HUSBAND AND EVERYTHING WAS LIGHT BETWEEN US. We were engaged in a respectful and moving act, and it allowed a sacredness to pass through me. Maybe this was what "sexual relations" really meant.

I grasped the entirety of that moment: here was the man I loved so much, a good man, a genuine partner. We had been through so much together, had done so much for each other. I didn't know how much longer we would have to spend our lives side by side, but we were both healthy, and this was the gift of that moment. When I really managed to grasp that, I burst into tears.

It had been many weeks since I cried. I had been so collected. But at that moment, all my pent-up emotions came out. I hadn't cried like that since giving birth, when I was still a sack of hormones. After all, I was out in the working world again, and in a functioning society hormones had to be repressed. The crying escalated to weeping.

"What's the matter?" Alon asked, confused and concerned in equal measure.

"I love you... I love you so much," I said while sobbing, and as we both continued moving our bodies and having sex, a peace settled between us. Every moment became softer, the boundaries between our bodies blurred and the more we became one body, the more I cried.

At one point my crying became so loud that Alon worried it would wake up Lavie, so he put his hand over my mouth. Somehow I found that funny, and my crying turned into uncontrollable laughter. I laughed and laughed—a laughter that was much louder than my crying.

We followed the rhythm of our bodies. At one point, Alon came, and a few moments later, I did too. I was complete presence. I was love. I looked at him. The whole room was red by candlelight, and in the backdrop of the curtains. We stayed inside each other for a long while, I can't say how long, because time had drifted away against that delicate presence.

At one point, Alon pulled out of me and went to shower. I remained lying in bed, wanting to treasure that moment, that connection that exists between man and woman. While feeling the fluids mix inside my body, I thought: how amazing that this substance is the stuff of life.

The responsibility for changing the relationship between the sexes is collective. It is critical that we stop the violence, that we allow men and women to connect to the life force inside them, that we rediscover the love of men for women, of women for men, and allow that love to lead the way.

OUR WORK MUST BE CONDUCTED IN PARALLEL: THROUGH MEN'S CIRCLES, WOMEN'S CIRCLES AND JOINT CIRCLES OF MEN AND WOMEN.
Over the last few years, as part of my work with large organizations, academic institutions and private individuals around the world, I have created content and safe spaces for men and women to explore healthy communication and joint development. The breakthroughs I have witnessed in these spaces remind me that, while significant work still lies ahead, a new reality is already un-

derway. There is a critical mass of men and women around the world willing to dedicate themselves to healing and rectification.

Also, in the purely female spaces that I have been fortunate enough to lead, a great hope has awoken in me. Every time I witness the leadership of a woman when she connects to her body, my initial realization as I set out on this receives further confirmation: there is something about the unique love that exists in our bodies as women that the world needs, and the only way for us to tap into it is to remember the original purpose of our bodies' role.

Our body is not a commodity, it is a compass that can reveal the way, a temple that must be tended to and whose needs must be met; it is our connection to life and contains all the resources we need in order to cope. There is nothing more revolutionary we can do for the status of women in the world than build an awareness of this.

In too many homes around the world women suffer abuse and decisions that compromise their bodies. While we battle discrimination and violence, our responsibility as free and privileged women is also to take a one hundred and eighty degree turn in our relation to our bodies and, by doing so, change this socio-cultural reality for the next generation.

What would a society look like in which women are encouraged to listen to their bodies, and express themselves accordingly? Let us remember how that feels, create curriculums that instill it, and invent products that encourage it — develop apps, initiate social events, create relevant virtual content — giving birth to work that reminds us what the path of the body really is.

We were born through the body, and through the body we can be reborn.

The moment we give preference to our body and its needs in the bedroom, we also give preference to our honest opinions and burning ideas in the conference room. Men and women across the globe are waiting to realize the unique solutions that women can bring to society. In politics, business, educational and cultural institutions, an invisible billboard is blinking red: *Present women wanted urgently!*

Being a present woman is being connected to your body and agreeing to love it in pleasure and in pain, and to embrace the parts you still have a hard time looking at.

It's agreeing to soar to the highest heights and sink to the lowest depths.

It's dreaming the biggest dreams and admitting to failure.

It's speaking your deepest desires without apologizing.

It's taking your place at the table and voicing your opinion even when it's not the popular one.

It's putting an end to the lies.

It's learning to accept.

It's taking risks.

It's acknowledging that we are part of the world, and that we have the ability to influence society, earn money, and assume positions of power.

It's realizing that we are living through complicated, uncertain times, and that now is the time to find solutions that will secure a healthy existence for our children's sake.

It's doing things jointly and jointly conquering our ego-related fears and jealousies when facing each other.

It's loving men and collaborating with them.

Female leadership is not sufficient for a good life on Earth, just as male leadership isn't. We need both.

Our mutual dependency is the wheel around which the world's axis revolves, and although I am terrified of this wheel's movement, it is what I live for.

I'M SCARED OF THE DAY WHEN PEOPLE I LOVE WILL DIE AND LEAVE THEIR BODY. Just like that.

I'm afraid we won't be able to meet anymore, feel our bodies, talk to our hearts and make each other's eyes dance with words. Some thinkers have posited that at one point we can stop identifying, release our attachment and realize we are no longer our bodies. My work here is the exact opposite. Each time I try to increasingly accept how much I am my body, how all-encompassing and knowing it is. The more I grow, the more I choose to attach myself to life here on Earth, inside a flesh-and-blood body, deeply identifying with the stories of my life and inextricably linked to the people who are with me. I'm nothing without them.

I imagine myself standing in front of my sisters, parents, husband or children, and I cry out of love for them; with every tear that falls something falls away—literally. First my nose crumbles, then my mouth, my hands; my limbs become a line. My eyes remain, still brimming with tears, until they too are no more. I have no body. I have become water. Something in me is aware that it is only through the body that I know love, but the more I dissolve into it, the more this body will disappear. The paradox of life and death.

* * *

Just as I finished writing the book, I saw two Whatsapp messages from Alon.

The first said "get." The second: "back to me."

He thinks he was referring to a missed call, but I know that he was asking me not to leave the here and now.

Stay with me in body, his expression asks of me every day. And for the time being, I consent.

DEAR READERS,

It has been two years since I published "Present Woman" in Israel and I have already received thousands of letters from women and men alike who have been moved by the book and inspired to embark on a journey of their own. A journey towards the body, healing relationships, self-fulfillment, and exploring new realms.

Last year, my daughter Agam was born. Every day, as I gaze into her eyes, I am encouraged to delve deeper into the present woman that I am, to expand the movement of present women and men, and to awaken the relationships with our bodies.

If there is someone in your life who is ready for this journey, I invite you to give them this book. To pass on the message of the "Present Woman."

In the following pages, you can read about additional places where you can meet brothers and sisters on the journey of the body. For now, I will conclude with a prayer I wrote for Agam, dedicated to every girl and boy in the world:

"May I be everything for you that I couldn't be for myself. May you find joy in being a woman, may you love your body, may you choose people who are good for you. May your voice be heard without interference. May you never feel ashamed. Today, I am 35 years old, and I still feel ashamed to shine with my full light. I still feel guilty when I take up too much space, still sometimes feel uncomfortable receiving. May you not waste energy on breaking glass ceilings or harboring doubts about your sexuality.

May you soar in your life and take us with you to the highest heights. May this be the generation of girls and boys who have come into the world through us, carried in our wombs, but who will actually be the ones to raise us. Raise us to choose to be great and from that place, to join men in a meeting of the minds. In courageous partnership, in mutual learning, in healthy and loving relationships."

Thank you for joining our movement.

Yours, Narkis

APPENDIX:
SPACES TO VISIT AFTER READING

I love books, but I love people even more and the creations that are woven through our relationships. I've created these spaces and topics for us to explore on a daily basis. You are invited to join:

1. "PRESENT WOMEN"

The digital workbook (accessible via the QR code below) invites you to explore your story, or parts of it, while or after reading the book. From my experience with women's circles and digital spheres, sharing our story is like going through a version upgrade, and facilitates healing. When we bring these stories to light, we allow others to do the same. Scan the QR code, participate in the exploration process and join the group we have started. The creation of value is collaborative, as are the fruits we reap together.

Men, you're also invited.

Scan the QR code for a detailed explanation.

www.narkisalon.com/booklet-en

2. "PLAYING WITH FIRE"

A space that invites honest, direct and intense dialogue conducted by women and men about sexuality, relationships and life itself. Through the podcast and the group, we seek to show how the world could look when women are turned on to their lives with male attentiveness and support, and when men are connected to their vulnerability and tenderness through female attentiveness and containment. We strive for a world in which, from a position of strength and vulnerability, we begin a process of peace between the sexes, with women and men directing their gaze at explosive topics in order to advance our society.

In the group, brave women and men discuss topics of sexuality, relationships, love, fears and dreams with radical sincerity.

To join the group, go to the QR below. The group is conducted in Hebrew, with posts translated into English via Facebook. Joining is free. Just answer a questionnaire beforehand and follow the rules.

3. DOUBLE YOU

A network of female entrepreneurs from across various fields: politics, business, social initiatives, art and more. What they share? a commitment to embody and inspire female leadership around the world that encompasses the body, emotions, mind and soul. The network holds meetings in biannual workshops that allow participants to delve deeper into a journey towards holistic female leadership, where the "red tent" meets the business plan. Double You's community members also offer empowerment and mentoring programs for at-risk girls.

For more details and collaborations, visit our website: www.doubleyou.life

4. FOR COLLABORATIONS, LECTURES, WORKSHOPS AND SHARING WILD IDEAS FOR OTHER ENDEAVORS, visit my website and contact me. You can also find more resources there: www.narkisalon.com

Or write me at: contact@narkisalon.com

ACKNOWLEDGMENTS AND RECOMMENDATIONS

It took me three years to publish this book, and without all the people who accompanied me, even thirty years wouldn't have been enough.

First, I'd like to thank the circle that surrounds me every day: Alon, Lavie, Agam, my parents, my sisters and my companions in the ever-growing Double You tribe. Without you I have no why.

A big thanks to my closest friends, you know who you are. Thank you for accepting me the way I am, thank you for encouraging me, thank you for setting things straight when I get confused, thank you for the great privilege of being alongside you.

Thank you to the Inys, Alon's family. You have become my second family, opening your house and hearts to me every weekend anew.

Thanks to the amazing team that leads Playing with Fire with me. Every day we face complex questions that open more room in our hearts. A big TODA to Hila Steinitz Namdar, for supporting me in everything I do with your huge heart and beautiful mind.

I am also grateful for the people that are supporting my consciousness; your reflections, your truth and integrity are illuminating my journey: Stav Peter, Anat Avinach, Amoz Batz and more.

Thanks to all the people who have accompanied me professionally from start to finish as I originally wrote this story in Hebrew, one layer after another.

Adi Rosenberg, the pioneer. In many respects, your support is what motivated me to set out on a path I've been longing for since the first grade.

To Noa Bareket. I got butterflies in my stomach when you responded to my wooing and they continue flapping their wings every time I read one of your texts. Thank you for midwifing me through the Hebrew editing.

To Ron Dahan for his directness, depth and courage in the editing that brought this book into its final form.

To Maya Kaynan for her professional proofing and patience with all my mix-ups!

To Amit Noyfeld for the support in the publication. To the talented Tom Lahat, for the cover design and endless video chats about it. To Hani Ben Aharon, for the design, layout and printing. To Stephanie Knoppel for the amazing illustrations, which helped me understand the book on another level, and for connecting me with Yulia Oz Damir.

To Neta Kerzner for the cover and Alon Gerzon Raz for the customer service. And to Shir Marom and Neta for their brainstorming sessions. To Daniel Shenar and Inbal Arieli, who were attentive and responded to every question.

To all the people who read with an eye toward offering feedback and help: Aya Achimeir, Daniel Shani, Karin Levi, Dafna Arad, Natalie Rosenboim, Nilli Alon Donner (both are my biological sisters!), Leigh Ofer (who also assisted with translations into English), Daniel Goldstein, Michaela Lahat, Shachar Berlovitz, Arava Gerzon Raz, Matan Hakimi and Michael Shurp, Daniela Zamir — your generosity, love and wisdom made the manuscript all the richer.

To Leanne Raday who originally translated this book to English- thank you for all your patience and curiosity in unleashing my story; to Tobye Hananel for supporting the editing process with such dedication; to Dalia Rosenfeld- you are a magician, thank you for capturing my voice through your edits. A huge thanks from my heart to the sisters who supported me in igniting this conversation in America: Jess Jacobs, Nicole DeLaRosa, Tal Waksal ,Rachel Goldstein, Ella Tamar Adhanan, Orka Teppler and Michal Ansky. Together we are creating new models of feminine partnerships.

Many thanks to the people in the literary industry who offered help and support. Your knowledge and experience were invaluable and saved me a lot of time.

A special thanks to people in the industry who completly ignored me: I won't mention your names because you might think I'm being sarcastic, but in your dismissal of me you invited me to acknowledge myself and to grow as a writer.

Thank you to all the teachers and companions from whom I have learned about the path of the body over the years. Thank you for being pioneers in this field, thank you for maintaining your integrity, thank you for improving all the time. Unfortunately, as in many other fields, the field of studying and treating through sexuality around the world also includes people who lack experience and fail to take responsibility for the safety of the spaces they facilitate. There are workshops and festivals that are platforms for predators and cause damage to people's relationships with their bodies. If you're curious and would like to join a workshop or try therapy, I recommend receiving recommendations from people you trust and deciding if this path is for you.

I had planned to add a list of all the superb teachers and therapists in Israel in the field, but then realized that I cannot offer recommendations without knowing the recommendees. Again, I suggest doing your research before deciding and I hope the resources offered at the end of this book may help you in that task.

However, the main objective of this book isn't to send you to sex therapy or a sexuality workshop, but to invite you to set out on the path of the body, which differs for each of

us, and to encourage you to share your personal story. From my experiences with the groups I facilitate, I witness every day anew how our stories give us freedom, understanding and insight into ourselves and others.

A huge thanks to all the storytellers: To those who read, react, contribute to the communities and extensive content channels we share. For the most part, we have no personal acquaintance, but on some level we live our lives together and influence each other through the written word.

Last but not least, I'd like to thank myself. For finding the courage to publish, for rising above the excuses, demons, waves of sadness and doubt. For making this transition. We have never had (you and I) a greater pleasure than writing.

Now it's your turn to write. I can't wait to read.

See you on the other side.

Scan the QR code for a detailed explanation.

www.narkisalon.com/booklet-en

Made in the USA
Columbia, SC
19 September 2023